When Spencer tugged her ever so slightly to face him, Raina saw the sexy gleam lurking in his dark brown eyes.

She knew she should resist what she knew was about to happen, but she didn't.

Spencer's head descended toward her and he brushed his lips briefly but firmly across hers. His lips were featherlight yet determined as they caressed hers, and a soft sigh escaped her lips. He threaded his fingers through her wavy curls and her lips parted of their own accord. His tongue slipped inside her warm and waiting mouth and explored the recesses of her mouth, filling, learning and savoring every inch of her. He devoured her with his seductive kiss in such a possessive and primitive way that it left Raina wanting more.

Raina had to force herself to push Spencer away even though her lips still tingled from his kiss. His heat and breath against her face overwhelmed her. "Oh, my God!"

What the hell was she doing? Spencer could have been with Alexa! She'd gotten caught up in the moment and allowed herself to let go, and look what had happened. He'd been seducing her all day with his charms and she'd fallen prey to them like an innocent schoolgirl. "That kiss should never have happened."

"I disagree," he whispered, so the other family couldn't hear. "That kiss has been in the making since the moment I laid eyes on you. I've wanted to know if you would taste as sweet as you looked and you didn't disappoint."

Books by Yahrah St. John

Harlequin Kimani Romance

Never Say Never
Risky Business of Love
Playing for Keeps
This Time for Real
If You So Desire
Two to Tango
Need You Now
Lost Without You
Formula for Passion
Delicious Destiny
A Chance With You

YAHRAH ST. JOHN

is the author of ten books and numerous short stories. A graduate of Hyde Park Career Academy, she earned a bachelor of arts degree in English from Northwestern University. Her books have garnered four-star ratings from *RT Book Reviews*, Rawsistaz Reviewers, Romance in Color and numerous book clubs. In 2012, St. John was nominated for *RT Book Reviews* Reviewers' Choice Award for Best Series Romance. A member of Romance Writers of America, St. John is an avid reader of all genres. She enjoys the arts, cooking, traveling, basketball and adventure sports, but her true passion remains writing. St. John lives in sunny Orlando, the City Beautiful.

A
CHANCE
WITH
You

YAHRAH ST. JOHN

HARLEQUIN® KIMANI™ ROMANCE

To my girlfriends and sisters: Dimi, Therolyn,
Tiffany and Tonya.

Recycling programs
for this product may
not exist in your area.

ISBN-13: 978-0-373-86326-6

A CHANCE WITH YOU

Copyright © 2013 by Yahrah Yisrael

For questions and comments about the quality of this book, please contact us
at CustomerService@Harlequin.com.

Printed in U.S.A.

www.Harlequin.com

Dear Reader,

I came up with Raina and Spencer's story several years ago after I'd watched the movie *No Reservations* and saw current athletes in paternity pickles, but it was put on the back burner. When I finally sat down to write their story, the words flowed.

Raina losing her sister and gaining custody of her niece while falling for basketball great Spencer was the easy part. Crafting a story containing grief, family duty and custody while still being true to their spicy romance was a bigger challenge, but I rose to the occasion. Raina was a workaholic much like me; add in sexy reformed bad boy Spencer on the path to redemption and voilà, a sexy romance is born.

Be sure and visit my website at www.yahrahstjohn.com for the latest news or contact me via email at Yahrah@yahrahstjohn.com.

Kind regards,

Yahrah St. John

Thank you to my beau Freddie Blackman,
friends Tiffany Griffin, Dimitra Astwood,
Therolyn Rodgers, Tonya Mitchell, Denise Mose,
Kiara Ashanti and Bhushan Sukhram and last, but not
least, my dad, Austin Mitchell, and my family the
Mitchells, Bishops, Smiths and Astwoods for believing
that my creativity has the potential for greatness.
Hugs to my loyal readers for all their support.

Prologue

"Are you sure you want to leave Zoe with me?" Raina Martin asked her twin, Alexa. She was stunned by her sister's bequest that she be given sole guardianship of her six-year-old daughter, Zoe. She was single, after all, and her five-year-old catering business was finally taking off.

"Of course." Alexa smiled weakly at her sister from her hospital bed at Jackson Memorial. She'd been fighting off a rare cervical cancer for over a year, and she was exhausted. Raina knew she was tired of the chemo and radiation and was ready for nature to take its course. "You're the only person I trust to take care of my baby."

"What about Mom and Dad?" Raina looked toward the door that their parents had just gone through to get a cup of coffee. Their parents, Crystal and Anthony Martin, were financially secure and lived in a huge four-bedroom house with a swimming pool. They could easily take care of Zoe. "You know they would be up to the task."

"Would they love and care for her? Yes, but would they be the fun-loving parent that I know you will be?" Alexa inquired, shaking her head. "I doubt that."

"I'm honored that you trust me enough to take care of her," Raina replied, touching her chest. "But…" Her voice trailed off. She didn't know how she would manage taking care of herself and Zoe and running her thriving business, but somehow she would. It was Alexa's dying wish. Losing her was like losing a part of herself.

"Don't doubt yourself like you always do," Alexa stated. Her twin had never been bold; that trait had been her strength. "You have what it takes, Raina."

"Oh, Alex…" Raina started to cry. Her sister's optimism for life was what she would miss the most. Alexa always saw the glass as half-full and encouraged Raina to go after what she wanted, even if that meant leaving her cushy gig as an executive chef at a fine dining establishment in favor of starting up a catering business. How was she going to go on without her and be strong for Zoe? Zoe would be grieving and would need a mother. Raina barely knew how to take care of herself.

"Don't worry. I know you're up to the task," Alexa said. "It's because of you that I even had Zoe."

Alexa had been a wild child from the start, always sneaking out to meet boys and going out to parties. When she'd gotten pregnant, she hadn't been sure what to do, but Raina had told her what a blessing her child would be and had promised to support her—and she had. Their parents had been terribly disappointed, but as soon as they'd seen their granddaughter, they'd fallen in love.

"Yes, but what about Zoe's father?" Raina inquired. Alexa had never spoken of him, and Raina had never pushed for his identity until now. She had to know. What about child support?

"He…he won't be issue," Alexa said, coughing uncontrollably.

At her vague response, Raina realized the reason Alexa had never mentioned him and what she'd always suspected. "He has no idea he has a child, does he?" She stared into her twin's dark brown eyes. The man hadn't even shown up when Zoe had been born. As far as she knew, he'd never met his daughter.

"Please, Raina." Alexa's coughing continued.

"Take a deep breath, okay?" Raina wiped Alexa's brow with the damp cloth lying on the nightstand and sat down on the hospital bed to hold her sister's hand.

"Can't you just let this drop?"

Raina shook her head. "No, I can't. What if, God forbid, something happens to Zoe and I need him for medical reasons? What if Zoe wants to get to know him one day? You have to tell me, Alexa."

"Raina…" Alexa began wheezing.

Raina could feel her sister starting to drift, but she couldn't let her die without an answer. "I need to know, please," she begged.

"Purse." Alexa pointed to the nightstand drawer that held her belongings. Raina went over, pulled out her handbag and rushed over to the bed. Alexa sat up as best she could. Summoning strength, she reached inside and pulled out a tattered photo, then handed it to Raina.

"Spencer. Spencer Davis will help you," Alexa said, handing Raina the photo.

"Thank you." Tears began to fall in earnest from Raina's eyes as she watched her sister drop back onto the pillows and succumb to the cancer she'd been fighting for so long. "I promise you I will take excellent care of Zoe."

"I know you will," Alexa replied. "That's why I can die knowing she has you by her side. Tell Mom and Dad that I love them."

"I will." Raina wiped the tears away with the back of her hand. "I love you, Alexa."

"Tell…Zoe," Raina whispered, "that I love her and that—" she took a long tortured breath "—she was the light of my life."

Raina nodded and reached across the bed to close her sister's eyes. "Goodbye, Alexa." Raina lowered herself onto her sister's lifeless body and wept.

Chapter 1

"Zoe, hurry up or we'll be late for school," Raina said, looking around the living room for her car keys.

They'd overslept because she'd come back late from a catering gig and fallen asleep on the couch, which meant she hadn't heard her alarm going off.

Raina glanced at herself in the mirror as she quickly put her unruly wavy hair into an unflattering ponytail. She could thank her German mother and African-American father for her café-au-lait-colored skin, naturally thick mass of long curls and almond-shaped eyes. She attributed her slim physique to her mother, who was naturally thin and had been a model in her youth, and her father, a former military man who followed a rigid exercise plan. Both her parents were vegetarians, so it was funny when she turned out to be a meat-loving carnivore who ran her own catering business.

"C'mon, Zoe." Raina snapped up the keys from the end table and rushed down the hall to Zoe's room. Zoe was still packing her book bag on her bed and going at a snail's pace.

Raina rushed over to help her, throwing books into a book bag. "I told you to pack your bag last night."

"I know, but I forgot," Zoe said, looking up at Raina with sad eyes. Her niece was her splitting image, possessing the same wavy hair and café au lait skin. The only difference was she had Alexa's spitfire personality, which was evident by her outfit of a bright fuchsia print T-shirt, jeans and pink flats.

Raina sighed and took a deep breath. It wasn't Zoe's fault she was rattled this morning. She just had to be more prepared for their morning ritual; she had to act and think like a mother. Not that she exactly knew what that meant. Sure, she'd had Zoe overnight the odd night or two while Alexa was alive, but that was completely different than being responsible for her care 24/7.

So much had changed in the past three months since Alexa had died and left guardianship of Zoe to Raina. She'd moved Zoe into the home that she'd bought after her catering firm had acquired several large contracts to cater parties for an advertising agency. After those contracts were finalized, the business had flourished. She'd been so busy, she hadn't found the time to follow up on the piece of information her sister had given her before she'd died, which was that Spencer Davis could help her. Raina was sure Alexa had meant he was Zoe's father.

And it was time she finally did something about it.

Just the other day, Zoe had mentioned she wished she had a dad like other kids. But what should Raina do about it? Show up at his doorstep with Zoe in hand and confront him? There was no easy way to tell a man he had an illegitimate daughter he knew nothing about. Her parents had advised her to consult an attorney. Raina was a nonconfrontational kind of woman, and she didn't relish going down that avenue, but Spencer Davis had a responsibility to his daughter, her niece.

As she and Zoe drove the short distance to her elementary school, Raina resolved to take action and soon.

"So how's Miss Zoe this morning?" Summer Newman, Raina's business partner and childhood friend, asked when Raina came rushing through the kitchen door of their catering shop a half hour later.

"Forgetful as usual." Raina sighed, grabbing her apron off a nearby hook and wrapping it around her middle. "Sorry I'm late, but Zoe hadn't packed her book bag this morning and she'd forgotten her lunch on the counter and didn't tell me until we got to the school, so I had to go back home to get it."

Raina glanced apologetically at Summer. She wasn't surprised her bohemian friend was dressed in a colorful coral-and-teal maxi-dress that reached her ankles. A scarf of the same pattern was secured over her shoulder-length dreads. She was also wearing one of her colorful assortment of aprons.

"It's okay, Raina," Summer responded. "No one expects you to get this motherhood thing right all at once." She returned to chopping the trinity of onions, peppers and celery.

Raina's gaze clouded with tears and she immediately sank onto a bar stool across from Summer. "Thanks…

It's just that I feel like I'm doing such a bad job. And Zoe needs me to have it together."

"Give yourself time." Summer stopped what she was doing and stared at Raina. "Alexa sprung this unexpectedly on you. You always thought your parents would raise Zoe."

"But she *chose* me instead." Raina touched her chest. "She trusted me. I just don't want to screw this up." She sighed. "How did Alexa do this all alone for six years?"

Summer shook her head. "I don't know. Growing up, Alexa couldn't have been further from mommy material."

Summer had met the Martin twins during the third grade. Raina and Alexa couldn't have been more different, and Summer had immediately clicked with Raina. Raina was warm and kind, while Alexa had been self-involved and arrogant until she'd gotten pregnant. Suddenly, the world had been turned on its axis and Alexa morphed into a dedicated mother and compassionate human being, volunteering for parent events at Zoe's school and selling cookies for Girl Scouts.

Meanwhile, Raina began focusing more on herself rather than keeping Alexa out of trouble. Raina and Summer started their catering business, Diamonds and Gems Catering, five years ago, and after a few false starts had turned their once struggling business into a success, thanks to word of mouth in the right circles in Miami.

"I know—isn't it crazy?" Raina asked. "But all of a sudden, once Alexa found out she was pregnant this mama bear came out of nowhere. It took me completely by surprise."

"And yours is in there somewhere, too." Summer

gave Raina a confident smile. "But in the meantime, it wouldn't be a bad idea to find Zoe's father. He should be helping you during this difficult transition. I mean Alexa didn't get pregnant by herself."

"This is true," Raina acknowledged, nodding her head in agreement. "My parents have been telling me that I should hire an attorney and request this Spencer Davis submit to a paternity test."

"Sounds like sage advice."

"I just hate to put this man on the defensive from the start when I need his help," Raina replied. "I know he has a responsibility to Zoe, but my sister wasn't blameless, either. She never told him she was pregnant."

"But how else can you get him to agree to a paternity test?" Summer asked. "Most men aren't going to take one voluntarily."

"I suppose you're right," Raina said. "I just thought I could reason with him, but I guess that's unrealistic. I will go see the attorney in the morning."

"Good girl. Now if you don't mind, we need to make the hundreds of canapés for our event tomorrow. Otherwise, we'll never be ready in time."

"Let's get to work." Raina sighed.

"Lloyd, my friend," Spencer Davis said into the phone as he propped his long legs on the cherrywood desk in front of him. "You know you're going to have to come higher on your offer. Derrick Quinn is the star of the team, and, as you know, he's a free agent at the end of this season...."

Spencer let his sentence trail off. As a successful sports agent, he was in a position of power. He'd found that a key talking point was implying the star player

would look elsewhere, and soon owners came around
to seeing things his way. He listened as Lloyd tried to
backtrack, but it was a losing battle. Spencer was not
settling for anything less than the best for his client.

Since retiring from basketball four years ago after a
successful fifteen-year run with the Miami Falcons, he'd
opened his own sports agency and quickly signed two
of his former teammates to his roster. He'd opened up
a small office in downtown Miami that overlooked the
bay. And soon his reputation for fair and honest dealing had helped catapult his starter agency into one of
the premier agencies along the East Coast.

"Well, I appreciate that, Lloyd," Spencer returned.
"And I look forward to hearing from you with a better
counter." He hung up the phone and rose from his seat.
From his doorway, he peeked out and looked at his assistant, Mona Dean.

She smiled when she saw him. Spencer knew the
older woman had a soft spot for him. It was probably his
six-foot-four height, although to most he was short for a
basketball player. In his heyday, Spencer had been quite
the ladies' man. Women of all ages had flocked to him,
eager to spend time with a three-time NBA champion.
What he liked most about Mona was that she'd been a
happily married woman for twenty-five years. And she
knew how to give him hell when needed.

"Don't I have lunch with Ty scheduled for noon
today?" he inquired.

"Yes, but I made the reservation for half an hour
later since Mr. Wilson is always notoriously late for
your lunches."

His best friend, Ty Wilson, was also a former NBA
star who'd been drafted to play for Atlanta. Although

they'd played on opposing teams for years, they'd developed a rapport when they'd been on the U.S. Olympics basketball team years back and won gold. They'd been friends ever since. Every time Ty was in town to visit his family, they got together to catch up on each other's lives and reminisce about old times. Spencer looked forward to their gatherings.

He laughed heartily. And the woman was meticulous, too. "Thank you, Mona. Just send him in when he arrives."

Spencer returned to his desk, but he stopped when the glare from the window shone a light on a framed photograph of Spencer, Ty and his younger brother, Cameron, who'd died nearly four years earlier. Seeing the photograph brought back a smile to Spencer's lips but his heart broke for what could have been avoided.

The three of them had been inseparable during the off-season of the NBA. They'd traveled together, partied together, drank together and, worse, done drugs together. After a record number of incidents with the authorities, Spencer had realized they were on a downward spiral and stated they should clean up their act. Ty had agreed, and once he'd met Brielle and gotten whipped, he'd been totally on board. But Cameron, Cameron wouldn't, *couldn't* stop.

Spencer had unsuccessfully tried to get Cameron into AA, but he'd stubbornly refused. "I have control of this," Cameron would say. "I'm a two-time NBA champion. I know discipline." But he'd been wrong. *Dead wrong.*

When Cameron's team had tanked the Eastern Conference, Cameron had been distraught. He'd viewed it as his last chance to get a "three-peat," and he'd gone on a drinking binge. Spencer had accompanied him, appointing himself as the designated driver to ensure Cameron made it safely back home. But in a sad twist of fate, their car got involved in an accident that claimed Cameron's life and left Spencer with survivor's guilt.

"Mr. Davis, Ty is—" Before Mona could finish the sentence from the intercom, Ty came bursting into his office with an abundance of energy. Spencer rose immediately to greet him, instantly throwing off the sorrow he was beginning to surrender to before Ty's visit.

"What up, my man?" Ty came forward and grasped Spencer in a bear hug, patting his back. "You're looking well in your suit."

"Working hard," Spencer replied. "Trying to making a success of this agency." He spread his arms and motioned around the room.

"Word on the street is you've got some of those owners' noses wide-open."

Spencer chuckled. "Who better to know some of their antics than a seasoned vet such as myself."

Ty gave Spencer a warm smile. "No one better than you, Spencer. Let's go get some grub."

Thirty minutes later, he and Ty were seated at Area 31, the restaurant on top of the EPIC Hotel, and looking over the menu as they sipped on sparkling water. If it had been five years ago, they'd have ordered a bottle of champagne.

"You look good, Ty," Spencer commented, eyeing his best friend's jeans, white shirt and blazer. At six foot seven, all Ty's clothes had to be custom-made, which was why he was always smartly dressed.

"Well, it's all this clean living and good food," Ty replied, patting his ever-increasing waistline. "You know, no drinking and no drugs and of course Brielle. Meeting her really made all the difference."

Spencer nodded. Since meeting his second wife, Ty had kept his promise to refrain from all the drinking and drugs he'd abused during his basketball career and settled down to life as a sports anchor for a local TV station in Atlanta. The couple was also about to welcome their first child. "I'm really happy for you, Ty."

"I wish the same for you," Ty said, staring at him intently. "It's time for you to let go of the past, Spencer."

Spencer suspected Ty knew he still harbored a lot of guilt for what he thought he could have done to help his brother. "That's easier said than done."

"You did all you could for Cam. We both did," Ty replied. "You have to move on. Matter of fact, I think it's time you settle down."

"With who?" Spencer asked. "With the basketball groupies hanging around the arenas, ready to land them a pro player or a former one? You know how it is in the business. It's hard to meet anyone truly genuine and without any ulterior motive."

Ty nodded. "I hear you." Ty had got caught in that very same scenario with his first wife, who'd married him just for his money. It hadn't taken him long to cut her loose, but not before she'd taken him for a mint because he'd married her during one of his drunken escapades and without a prenuptial agreement. "But you can't give up, either. There has to be a good woman out there. I mean when was the last time you got laid?"

Spencer laughed at Ty's blunt question. "That's none of your business." He pointed in his direction. "But if you must know I've been celibate for a while. I just need to meet someone with substance, who I can hold an intelligent conversation with. You know anybody like that?"

"I'll ask Brielle if she has any friends," Ty replied. "But all I'm saying is that man was not meant to live alone."

"And as soon as a beautiful, smart woman walks into my life, I'll snap her up." Spencer snapped his fingers.

"You never know, she could be just around the corner," Ty stated. "Like at Allyson Peters's party tomorrow for Parkinson's Research."

"I'm not up for any rubbery chicken at a charity event."

Ty eyed him suspiciously, "It's for a good cause. And who knows? You might meet someone."

"A socialite?" Spencer rolled his eyes. "That's exactly who I don't need to meet."

"Just come. Brielle and I are going. And look at it this way. At least you won't be working until all hours of the night. Mona told me you leave here well after the sun goes down."

"And how would she know?"

"You do know Mona, right?" Ty raised an eyebrow. Spencer's assistant was sharp and nothing escaped her.

"Oh, all right, I'll go," Spencer reluctantly conceded. "But if I have a bad time, I'm blaming it all on you."

Ty smiled, happy that he'd gotten Spencer to see things his way. "Good. We'll have fun tomorrow night."

Raina drove Zoe to her parents' the following evening so they could babysit while Raina and Summer had their catering event. Her mind went back to her meeting with the family attorney earlier that day.

"This picture certainly isn't enough to establish paternity," the attorney had said. "But it can certainly show that your sister Alexa knew Mr. Davis. Do you have any other evidence?"

Although Raina had been unable to supply him with any other evidence, he'd promised to hire an investigator to look into her sister's past. He'd also indicated he would be sending a letter to Spencer requesting he either sign an Acknowledgment of Paternity or submit to a genetic test to establish paternity.

"What if he doesn't want to take a genetic test?" Raina had inquired.

"Then we take this matter to the court," the attorney had said. "Where he'll then be forced to submit to a genetic test. Either way, we'll get results. It's just easier for all parties if he submits voluntarily."

Raina had no idea how Spencer Davis was going to feel being served with paternity papers, but she had to know if Zoe's father would step up to the plate. She wanted her niece to experience life with two parents. As soon as the thought came into her mind, Raina realized the finality of it. She was Zoe's mother. She would be raising Zoe, potentially with Spencer, a man she knew nothing about other than what she'd read on the internet.

After the funeral, Raina had decided to look him up online. Initially, she'd been stunned by the negative press about Spencer Davis. He was a reformed bad boy who'd been known to womanize, drink and carouse with all sorts of bad fellows, and he'd exhibited the worst behavior in public. The tide had changed, however, and recent press had Spencer Davis leading the straight-and-narrow life. He'd retired and opened his own sports agency. He'd garnered a few big clients as

well as a few Olympic athletes. One thing was clear:
Spencer could easily afford child support.

But what if Spencer wasn't Zoe father? What if the
photo was a bad lead? Was she prepared to take care
of Zoe alone?

Her mind wasn't able to answer because she'd arrived
at her parents' home. Before she could open the back
door, Zoe had already unbuckled herself and jumped
out of the car, reminding Raina that she needed to be
more cognizant of the child safety locks.

Zoe raced up the steps and rang the doorbell. Raina
sighed as she popped open the trunk and pulled out
Zoe's overnight bag. Slinging it over her shoulder, she
grabbed her purse and headed toward the now open
front door.

In eager anticipation of her only grandchild, her
mother had swung open the door and swept Zoe into
her arms. Raina found them in the hallway and saw her
mother smothering Zoe's face with kisses.

"Hey, Mom," Raina said, closing the door behind her.

"Hi, hon." Her mother barely hazarded her a glance
as she removed Zoe's jacket and led her to the living
room, where her father was no doubt watching the
nightly world news.

"Hello to you, too," Raina said, following behind her.

Her mother and Zoe joined her father on the sofa and
snuggled together.

"Hey, baby girl," her father spoke first. He gave her
a quick smile before returning to his news program.

It was moments like this that reminded Raina of the
indifference she'd always felt from her parents growing up. They'd thought they were having one little girl,
Alexa, and had only been prepared for one child. Imag-

ine their surprise when the doctor had told them he
heard a second heartbeat during delivery and her mother
had gone into labor again to give birth to Raina four
minutes later.

And now that their favorite daughter had been taken
from them so suddenly, her parents seemed to have
gravitated to Zoe like bees to honey. They'd been surprised and deeply hurt when Alexa had indicated she
felt Raina would be a better parent for Zoe. They, like
Raina, had assumed Alexa was leaving custody to
them. They were the logical choice, not a single, career-
minded woman.

"Well," Raina said and shifted uncomfortably from
side to side at the doorway. "Here's Zoe's overnight
bag." She dropped the bag with an unapologetic thud
onto the floor. "I'll be by tomorrow to pick up Zoe for
Caroline's birthday party."

Even though she would be dog-tired after an evening
on her feet, cooking and serving, Zoe had a school-
mate's birthday party to attend, and Raina was determined to make more of an effort to integrate herself
into Zoe's life. Sometimes it seemed as if the child had
more social engagements than Raina.

Raina was so busy working on making her catering
business a success, she had little or no time to go out,
much less date someone seriously. Her last serious boyfriend had been two years ago. Eric Thomas had gotten so frustrated by Raina's long hours and her lack of
time for their relationship that he'd hightailed it after
six months, leaving Raina alone and celibate the past
two years. Now that she was a single mother, Raina's
prospects were going to be even less promising.

Her mother finally seemed to remember Raina was

still in the room and glanced up. "Yes, Raina. Don't worry about Zoe—we've got her tonight. And if you need me to take her to Caroline's party, just let me know."

Raina shook her head. "Oh no, I've got it." She was determined to prove to her doubtful parents that Alexa hadn't made the wrong decision when she'd chosen her as Zoe's guardian.

Raina glanced down at her watch. "Well, I gotta go." She looked across the room and gave her niece a pleading look. "Can your auntie have a kiss?" She bent down until she was nearly Zoe's height.

Zoe paused for what seemed like an eternity before hopping off her grandfather's knee and giving Raina a halfhearted hug.

Raina batted her eyes, refusing to let them tear up. Zoe considered her the disciplinarian. Her grandparents gave Zoe anything and everything she wanted, and she adored them. Raina rose. It just wasn't fair. "See you tomorrow." She gave her folks and Zoe a wave and made a quick exit. She was eager to go to a place where she knew she belonged, where she mattered. Her kitchen.

"What a great turnout for Parkinson's Research," Raina commented as she and Summer set up with their staff for one of the largest charity events of the Miami fall season.

They'd already arranged their stations earlier that day and brought all their preparations for the canapés they would serve throughout the evening. Diamonds and Gems Catering was collaborating on the event with Traci Todd, a thriving party planner. Traci had set up a classy affair complete with lighting, decorations and a band.

"I'll say," Summer said. She'd never been in the presence of such movers and shakers. She could tell from the way people were dressed in designer tuxedos and vintage gowns that these folks were ready to put down some serious cash for the cause. Their client Allyson Peters was one of the largest contributors, and her company was sponsoring a large team that would run in the Miami Marathon and Half Marathon in January. This event was a precursor to help raise awareness as well as funds. "How much do you think they'll raise?"

Raina shrugged as she set out individual portions of her signature steak house sushi roll—shaved prime rib, asparagus, horseradish mayo and arugula—on platters. Their temporary staff had shucked hundreds of oysters for Summer's raw bar of oysters on the half shell with a black pepper mignonette. Their client had requested small bites to be passed around by liveried waiters.

Summer and Raina worked in unison as they rolled out the first course of appetizers. They followed up the sushi and oysters with seared sea scallops, a blue crab cake and spicy lamb meatballs. The night was going smoothly. The fee on the event would cover Diamonds and Gems Catering expenses for the month.

Midway through the second course, Summer moved away from the table. "I'm going to the kitchen for more of the bacon cream sauce," she told Raina. "I'll be right back."

"I'll hold down the fort," Raina said, pushing a wayward strand of hair out of her face as she arranged the food perfectly on a plate. She didn't notice the two tall men and beautiful woman approaching her table.

"Good evening." Raina looked up to give them a warm smile. The color drained from her face as she recognized the person staring back at her. It was none other than Spencer Davis.

"So what do you have here?" Spencer inquired as he looked down at the platters of food.

Her mouth moved as if to speak, but no words came out. Raina licked her lips in frustration. How in the world had she come face-to-face with Zoe's father?

Chapter 2

Spencer stared at the beautiful creature with the almond-shaped brown eyes. She was really quite exquisite with high exotic cheekbones on a delicate face. A pile of wavy hair was curled into a neat bun on top of her head, which made her look slightly prudish but sexy nonetheless. Spencer watched her lick her lips in frustration and a jolt of awareness shot straight through him. He couldn't remember the last time he'd felt such an instant attraction to a woman.

She blinked at him several times before answering him in the sweetest voice he'd ever heard.

She motioned to one platter. "What I've prepared for you here is a drunken sea scallop with a beer-infused bacon cream sauce, a blue crab cake with sun-dried tomato aioli and a spicy lamb meatball with cucumber yogurt sauce."

"Hmm…" Spencer moaned at the description, and he watched her eyes grow larger in response. "Sounds delicious." He kept his gaze on hers and neither of them wavered until Ty coughed.

"My wife would like the scallop, and I would love to try the lamb meatball," Ty said, eyeing Spencer curiously. He could tell when his boy had his eye on a woman. And this woman, whoever she was, had captured his attention.

Raina smiled. "Absolutely." She handed him a meatball on a small plate, then passed Brielle a small plate with a large scallop on it, but not before sprinkling both with fresh parsley. "Enjoy."

"I'll have one of everything," Spencer said. At her questioning look, he added, "I'm a growing boy."

Without speaking, she handed him a plate of all her offerings.

"Thank you." Spencer nodded and reluctantly followed his friends, who'd stepped away from the table to enjoy the first course.

When he joined them several yards away at a small bar-height table, Ty wasted no time calling him out on his instant infatuation. "That was some sexual tension back there," Ty said, glancing back at the woman behind the table, who was talking to several other guests ready to taste her delicious creations.

"I don't know what you're talking about," Spencer lied.

Brielle laughed as she took a bite of scallop. "You're a terrible liar, Spencer. We both saw it. No, make that *felt* the attraction between you two."

Spencer shrugged. "She's a beautiful woman. What can I say?" He wanted nothing better than to know what kind of figure was beneath the oversize chef coat she was wearing.

"Get her number," Ty suggested.

"I can't." Spencer shook his head. "She's working."

"The night is still young," Ty responded. "As the evening ends, I'm sure the opportunity will present itself."

"What do you think, Brielle?" Spencer turned to Ty's wife.

"She was definitely affected by meeting you," Brielle said. "I think you have a shot."

"All right." Spencer pointed his finger at the two matchmaking culprits. "But if I'm turned down flat, I'll have no one to blame but you."

"You won't," Ty returned.

Spencer sure hoped not. For some reason, his gut told him that this woman was someone worth knowing.

"You look like you've seen a ghost," Summer said when she returned with more bacon cream sauce and platters of pork belly. Their second course consisted of pork belly with sweet potato pancake and black pepper shrimp with smoked gouda cheese grits.

Raina pulled Summer away from the tables so no one could hear them. "You will never believe who is here."

She still couldn't believe it herself. But she was staring at gorgeous Spencer Davis. The pictures she'd seen online did him little justice. And it wasn't just his stature. It was everything about him: the big bushy eyebrows, the broad nose, the full succulent lips and the sexy smile. Add his bravado, appealing masculine smell and the way he wore that three-piece suit and she was smitten.

"Is it a celebrity?" Summer looked over her shoulder. Although she couldn't ask for autographs, she could definitely write about it on their catering blog.

"No," Raina whispered. "It's Spencer Davis."

"Shut the front door!"

Raina shook her head. "I can't believe he's here. Over there." She inclined her head toward the trio standing nearby, munching on food and sipping champagne.

"Oh my Lord!" Summer touched her chest. "Does he know who you are?"

Raina shook her head. "No. I don't think he's been served yet by my attorney, but...I never expected this, to meet him in person. *Do you see how fine he is?*"

Summer leaned back and did a double take. "Mmm...I see your point. He is mighty fine, but what can you do? It's not like you planned this. We had no idea he'd be here tonight."

"Like he's going to believe that when he finds out who I am." Raina sighed. She couldn't believe her luck. "He'll think I was scoping him out."

"And he'd be wrong," Summer scolded. "The only reason you're pursuing this is to find out the truth. Who's to say he's even Zoe's father?"

"But why else would Alexa have a photo of her and Spencer together?"

Summer shrugged. "I don't know, and we don't have time to speculate. We have to finish this party. He probably won't even come this way again. Come on—we have more tables to serve."

Summer couldn't have been more wrong, because as the next course was served, Spencer Davis kept coming back to Raina's table for a taste. And each time Raina became more and more flustered by the attention Spencer was bestowing on her.

If she was serving another person, he would wait patiently until the line dissolved and he could speak with her for a few moments about each course. Any other time, it would have been harmless enough, a little flirtation between adults. But this time was different. *This* man could potentially be her niece's father and her attorney was about to serve him with legal documents requesting he submit to a paternity test. Raina highly doubted Spencer Davis would be so enamored with her if he knew what a royal pain she was about to become in his life.

When Spencer saw a lull at the beautiful woman's table he decided to make his move. "That pecan bread pudding with whiskey sauce was divine," he said when he returned to the table.

"Thank you." The woman smiled at him.

"You're welcome." Spencer extended his hand. "Spencer Davis."

Raina shook Spencer's hand. "Nice to meet you, Mr. Davis. Now, er, if you'll excuse me, I have to start to clean up."

Spencer blinked with bafflement. "Are you honestly not going to tell me your name?"

"I don't mix with patrons," Raina said. Her answer sounded logical.

Spencer looked around. "The party is wrapping up and after that I won't be your patron." He looked into her warm eyes. "I was hoping we could maybe grab a drink later, you know, get to know each other."

Raina swallowed. "I'm sorry, but that won't be possible."

"Why not?"

"There's lots to do, Mr. Davis. Some of us have to work hard for a living rather than throw a basketball around."

A smile ruffled Spencer's mouth. "So you know who I am?"

"I'm a native of Miami," Raina replied, her smile mirroring his larger one. "Of course I would know the great Spencer Davis. You're a legend in this town."

"I was hoping I was incognito and you would..." His voice trailed off and he turned to walk away, but the woman called out to him.

"Hoped what?"

"Want to get to know me for me," Spencer responded, turning back around to face her. "I guess that would be too much to ask."

The woman seemed to be surprised by his honesty and cocked her head to one side. "Sincerity is not too much to ask. And any other time, I would—" Raina cut herself off. "I have too much going on in my life right now."

Spencer stared at her, his eyes clinging to hers, analyzing her, inwardly pleading for friendship. Her eyes were wary and he wasn't sure why. "I understand. Another time?" he said and reluctantly walked away. He'd decided not to push, but somehow he would find out who the woman was.

"I'm so glad this night is over," Raina said as she and Summer packed up the company van with all their supplies.

"Yeah, that was a close call with you and Spencer Davis. He was really into you and kept coming back to our table all night."

"You're telling me," Raina replied. "Worse yet, he asked me out on a date."

"Really? When?" Summer stopped putting boxes in the van and turned to Raina.

"After you'd gone inside after dessert."

"And what did you say?" Summer helped Raina put the last few boxes in the van before shutting the door. She fished the keys out of her jeans pocket, unlocked the doors and she and Raina jumped inside.

"I turned him down of course. Refused to give him my name," Raina said, buckling herself into the passenger seat. "I can't go out with him, Summer. It's just a matter of time before he finds out who I am, and then all hell will break loose."

"At least you could have had a little fun before it did."

"No." Raina shook her head fervently. "I just courted disaster tonight and narrowly avoided it. I need to stay clear of Spencer Davis until the dust settles. Let our attorneys duke it out."

"Do you honestly think that's possible? This isn't about business. This is personal."

"I know, and meeting Spencer Davis tonight just made it more so."

Spencer woke up with a start. He was bathed in sweat. He dragged his hands over his short curly Afro. He'd had the same nightmare he'd been having on and off for the past four years. It was the same nightmare that, even after years of therapy, he just couldn't shake.

It was the helplessness, the regret, the guilt, that always greeted him the morning after one of his episodes. He could see himself pinned in Cameron's car while he stared at his brother, cut and bleeding on the hood. He'd been unable to help him because he'd been trapped by the steering wheel. By the time the ambulance had arrived, it was too late. Cameron had sustained massive internal injuries and hadn't survived.

Why hadn't he made Cameron wear his seat belt? Spencer should have insisted, but Cameron had been belligerent that night. Knowing Cameron could have survived if he'd been belted in had caused Spencer to retreat into himself the past few years.

Ty was right; he would have to let go of the past and start to live again. Up until yesterday, he hadn't been sure he was ready. The woman he'd met last night had him seeing the possibilities.

She hadn't just been beautiful, either. He'd seen her interacting with the guests and she'd been kind and patient. When an older woman had dropped her cane, she'd rushed over to help her from behind the table. It was that kind of simple action that told him she was someone special.

Which was why he'd made sure he'd found Allyson Peters to thank her for the invite and to ask for the name of the caterer who'd made the excellent food. Raina Martin of Diamonds and Gems Catering. Raina. It sounded lovely on his lips, and he hoped the lady herself would taste as good.

Throwing back the covers, Spencer rose naked from his bed to head into the shower. As the spray pelted his back, Spencer was determined to meet Raina again. This time she would not turn him down.

After sleeping in late the morning after the Parkinson's event, Raina should have woken up feeling refreshed. Instead she felt a sense of dread, and it wasn't because of the kid's party she was now driving Zoe to.

Meeting Spencer Davis had been a shock, one she hadn't been prepared for. And to make matters worse, she'd been attracted to him. As she'd fallen to sleep last night, she'd tried to convince herself that it was nothing, but deep down she knew it wasn't. She'd felt butterflies swarming in her belly each time he'd come near her table. And when he'd asked her out, she'd wanted to jump for joy, but she couldn't. She was in a quandary of wanting Spencer for herself but knowing that Zoe needed him more.

The thing was men like Spencer Davis were never interested in her. They wanted fun girls, like Alexa had been back in the day. They didn't want neurotic, workaholic girls like Raina. But Spencer had sparked a desire in her she'd never felt before. None of her past relationships had made her feel the way Spencer had with one look.

"Auntie Raina." Zoe was poking her arm. "You missed the turn."

"Sorry." Raina snapped out of her reverie. She'd missed the right turn onto Caroline's street. She had to snap out of this. She would never have a chance with Spencer. Once he found out her identity, he would keep her at arm's length.

Several minutes later, she pulled into the car-lined street. She found a parking space several doors down. This time, Zoe couldn't jump out because Raina had made sure to put on the child lock. Raina exited the vehicle, pulled the gift for Caroline out of the trunk and came around to open Zoe's car door.

Zoe wasn't too happy about being confined, but she didn't mouth off.

"Here's your gift for Caroline." Raina handed her the gift bag with the greeting card. She hoped the little girl would like the video game she'd gotten; Caroline's mother had noted it on the wish list. Raina had been shocked at how much parents spent on children's toys. The gift had cost over fifty dollars.

A Caucasian woman opened the door. "Zoe, welcome," she said. "Come on in. All the kids are in the back on the obstacle course. And you must be Raina." She leaned over to give Raina a quick hug as she entered the foyer. "So glad to meet you. I'm Cynthia Williams."

"Thanks for having us," Raina replied.

"I'm just happy Zoe could attend, given the circumstances," Cynthia whispered.

"Well, my parents and I are trying to keep things as normal as we can."

"Is that even possible?" Cynthia blurted out.

It was an honest question that most people might be afraid to ask, but Raina didn't mind. She appreciated that the woman wasn't walking on eggshells around her like most of the other parents. When she'd come to school with Zoe a week after Alexa's death, she'd seen the downcast looks, the pity stares. Lord knew what poor Zoe was going through. She knew kids could be cruel. "We're doing the best we can," Raina answered.

Cynthia touched her shoulder. "Well, if there's anything that I can do, babysitting and the like, please let me know. Alexa was always such a help with Caroline."

"Thank you. I appreciate the offer."

Raina stayed in the kitchen with the other parents, sipping coffee and eating coffee cake, while the kids played outside in the inflatable obstacle course complete with pop-ups, a slide and a tunnel. She didn't have much to share with most of the women in the room because they were married homemakers. There were only two single parents in the bunch. Most of them were sympathetic and offered words of wisdom here and there, but Raina quickly realized she had a long road ahead of her if she didn't have Spencer Davis to help her. She just hoped he wouldn't hate her too much, but she didn't have any choice. She had to know the truth.

"Spencer, Chad Gray is on the phone," Mona told him on Monday morning.

"Did he say what it was in regards to?" Spencer pressed the intercom button down.

"No, but if you'd like me to twenty-question him, I can," she replied in her usual Mona-like manner.

"That won't be necessary. I'll take it." Spencer reached for the receiver. "Chad, what can I do for you?"

"Well, as your lawyer I was served with a request for you to submit to a paternity test."

"What!" Spencer sat up in his ergonomic executive chair. "What the hell are you talking about?"

"Why don't you tell me?"

"There's nothing to tell," Spencer replied. He'd always been an advocate for safe sex. Even if a woman claimed she was on the pill, he didn't care; he still put on a condom. Always. He wasn't going to take the chance of becoming a father before he was ready.

"Are you sure about that?"

"Yes," Spencer stated emphatically. "Matter of fact, I've been celibate of late."

"Well this is going back seven years," his attorney replied.

Spencer became silent. Seven years ago, he'd been knee-deep into partying and alcohol. Although he always stressed safe sex, was it possible that one time he could have slipped? "Who is she?"

"Does the name Alexa Martin ring a bell?"

Spencer's mind wandered, trying to recall his heyday of partying in the clubs with Ty and Cameron. The memories were fuzzy, but the name sounded oddly familiar.

"What does she want?"

"It's more like what her sister wants."

"Why would her sister care about paternity?"

"Because Alexa Martin passed away and her sister, Raina, has guardianship of her daughter, Zoe Martin."

Raina. It couldn't be his Raina, could it? "What's the sister's name again?" But even as he asked the question, Spencer knew the answer. It was as if someone had just punched him in the gut.

"Raina Martin. She's petitioning you to submit to a paternity test on behalf of her niece."

Spencer's heart sank. Raina. The first woman in years that he'd been attracted to, the first woman in a long, long time that he'd thought didn't have an ulterior motive in meeting him. He'd been wrong.

Raina Martin had connived her way into catering a party that she knew he would attend. *For what? What had she hoped to gain?* Had she been looking to see if she could have the same chance with him her sister might have had? If so, she'd sure played it close to the vest, acting all sweet and innocent. She'd really duped him.

"Well, the name Alexa Martin doesn't ring any bells. I don't recall having sex with her."

"That's all fine and good, but you don't want to push this, Spencer. It could get real ugly if she decides to take her story to the press. She could do a real smear campaign on you. I did some research and Alexa recently died of cancer. Beating up on her grieving sister whose only trying to take care of her niece would shine a negative light on you, especially when your agency is taking off."

"So she's a do-gooder?" Spencer asked bitterly, upset with himself for liking the fact that she was raising her sister's kid.

"If you want to call it that. Quite frankly, you can put this whole matter to rest by taking the paternity test and ruling yourself out."

"That sounds reasonable enough, Chad, but what if I am the girl's father?" Spencer inquired. "What then?"

"Then you'd better be ready to pay up. Raina Martin is requesting child support and is open to visitation rights."

"Visitation rights?" Spencer said. "If I'm the father, why would I leave my child to be raised by someone other than me?"

"You're right. The courts do prefer to leave a child with the birth parents, but you didn't even know she existed. And listen, at this point, this is all purely conjecture. You need to take the test."

"I'll give it some thought," Spencer said and quickly hung up the phone. But he was going to do more than give it some thought. He was going to find Raina Martin and give her a piece of his mind for her deceptive ways. Allyson had given him Raina's business card and he was about the pay the lady a visit.

She may not be a gold digger, but she wasn't a saint, either. Why else would she have catered the very same party he was attending? There was more to the story and he intended to find out what.

"I think we have some really good ideas for the Hudsons' dinner party in South Beach," Raina told Summer as they sat down at the kitchen counter, writing out the menu for their next event later in the week.

"Yeah, yeah," Summer said. "So when are we finally going to talk about what's really on your mind?"

"What do you mean?" Raina's brow furrowed.

"Spencer Davis ring a bell?"

Raina rolled her eyes upward. "Do we have to?" She was doing her best to avoid thinking about the sexy former basketball star. But he'd never been far from her thoughts. The other night, she'd had an erotic dream about making love to him. Raina knew a man like Spencer would know how to please a woman until her toes curled.

"Yes, we do," Summer said, swinging her bar stool closer to Raina until she was inches away. "You can't deny how affected you were. I haven't seen you blush like that ever. You were a nervous wreck."

"That's the problem," Raina replied. "It should have never happened. I should have kept my distance."

"How would we know he'd be at a charity event for Parkinson's Research?"

"I doubt he'll see it like that. He'll probably think I had an ulterior motive."

"For what? To meet the man that might be your

niece's father. Oh, the horror!" Summer grasped her chest in mock terror. "You didn't do anything wrong. And if I recall, he kept coming back for more of your decadent delights."

Raina laughed at the innuendo. "Well, our food is the best!" She smiled at her best friend. "But right now he's getting served by my attorney, so I doubt he'll want to get to know me any further."

"I wouldn't say that," a masculine voice said from behind Raina. "In fact I'd like to know exactly why you think I'm your niece's father."

Raina's breath hitched and her skin colored to crimson. She looked to her best friend with pleading eyes, but Summer's eyes were large with alarm and she just shrugged her shoulders.

Reluctantly, Raina spun around on her stool to face Spencer Davis.

Chapter 3

"Raina Martin," Spencer said her name with a smile rather than the indignation Raina had expected.

"How did you find me?" Raina asked, her throat parched.

"You're not the only one who can locate people," Spencer replied. "You've made quite a reputation for yourself."

Raina frowned.

"In a good way." Spencer held up her business card. "Allyson gave me your card when I asked her for your info after such delicious canapés."

"Y-you sought me out?"

His dark eyes watched hers from across the room as he walked farther into the kitchen, filling the small space that housed stainless steel refrigerators, commercial stoves and an abundance of pots, pans and cutlery.

She knew she must have looked a wreck wearing a stained chef's coat and jeans with her hair in a ponytail.

"Does that surprise you?" he asked, raising a brow. "I did ask you on a date and you turned me down. And I don't take no for an answer. But then imagine my surprise when my attorney is served with paternity papers on the very same day I planned on contacting you."

"Umm…I—I'm just going to go to the store for some supplies," Summer said, pointing to the back door. Neither Raina nor Spencer turned to watch her grab her hobo purse and keys from a nearby hook and scurry out the door.

Raina swallowed the lump in her throat. "That must have come as quite a shock."

"Yes, it was. It was very disappointing."

"Why's that?"

"Because I thought you didn't have an ulterior motive like most women who meet successful athletes… former athletes."

"But you think I have one now?"

"Perhaps."

"And what would it be?"

"I haven't figured that out yet."

"Well, you'd be wrong. I don't have one," Raina replied, standing up to face him. When she did, Spencer towered over her and she was slightly awestruck.

"Why didn't you tell me who you were?"

"It was hardly the appropriate time or moment to tell you that I thought you'd slept with my sister and had fathered her child. Might have been in poor taste, don't you think?"

Spencer smirked. "Touché. But that begs the question—what do you want from me, Raina Martin?"

"It's quite simple. DNA," Raina replied honestly. "I need to know if you're Zoe's father. And if you are, then I'm looking for help raising your daughter. I never thought I'd be a single parent. Wasn't my heart's desire, you know? I...I never thought my twin would die." Raina's voice cracked. "B-But it was my sister's last wish that I take care of Zoe, and I'm doing what I think is best for her. She needs a father."

"And financial support?"

"Do you honestly think that all I'm after is your money?"

Spencer knew she wasn't, but he said, "I don't know. Most women are."

"Well, I'm not most women."

That's what he'd known the other night. It was why he'd sought her out. It was why the paternity wrinkle had put him in such a pickle. "And what if I'm not Zoe's father?"

"Then I'm back to the drawing board," Raina answered.

"And why do you think I am?"

Raina didn't answer. Instead, she went to her purse on the hook where Summer's had been. Where had she gone? Raina glanced around. She hadn't even seen her leave. Had she been so engrossed in Spencer Davis that she was that oblivious? Why was he having this kind of effect on her?

"Because of this." She pulled out the picture of Alexa and Spencer and shoved it at him.

Spencer took the photo from Raina's hand and their fingers touched for the briefest of seconds, sending an electric current running through Raina. She looked up at Spencer to see if he'd felt it, and it seemed as if he had; his eyes darkened ever so slightly. Raina stepped away quickly.

Spencer looked down at the photograph and saw himself with a beautiful woman who looked somewhat like Raina, with similar facial fixtures, but not exactly. "So you were fraternal twins?"

Raina nodded without speaking. Losing her twin had been like losing her other half and she still could hardly talk about Alexa without getting choked up.

"Where did you get this?" Spencer inquired, holding up the photo.

"Alexa handed the picture to me before she died at the hospital."

"And this is all the proof you have?"

"Do I need more?" Raina asked, peering at Spencer. He was looking at the photograph so intently. She was picking up on a vibe. "Do you recognize Alexa?"

Spencer nodded, "I remember kicking it with her, but that's all. And I definitely didn't sleep with her."

"How would you know?" Raina said, putting her hand on her hip, "According to the press, at the time you and your crew were quite the party animals. Do you even remember who you slept with?"

Spencer frowned. "Are you implying that I'm a slut puppy?"

Raina laughed at his description. "If the shoe fits."

"Then you're basically calling your sister one because she would have been nothing other than another groupie trying to entrap a basketball player. She wouldn't be the first and she certainly won't be last."

"How dare you!" Raina was horrified that he would speak of her deceased twin in such a fashion, and she turned away from Spencer immediately. His comment wasn't that far from the truth. During that time, she and Alexa had lost touch because Raina hadn't approved of Alexa's lifestyle.

"Listen, I'm sorry, Raina." He touched her shoulder, but she jumped away from him. "All I'm saying is that this photograph isn't proof enough that I slept with your sister and fathered a child. All it does is prove we went out once. But then again, I wasn't celibate back then, so I'll agree to your paternity test just so we can squash this and move on. *I know* I'm not Zoe's father."

Raina spun around on her heels. "How can you say that with such certainty? You clearly were no angel back then. And the internet said you were known to drink to excess. How do you know who you slept with?"

"Trust me when I say that I don't casually go to bed with a woman without protection. It's just not safe. And further, I would think your sister would have remembered sleeping with me and might have mentioned it."

"Because you're that unforgettable?" Raina asked, raising a brow. She was sure he was. Her female intuition told her that once Spencer Davis made love to a woman, she would never forget it.

Spencer walked toward her, grasped a few tendrils of Raina's hair and spun them around his finger. "Don't you think so?" he asked huskily, leaning over her.

Raina's breath caught in her throat and she couldn't find the words to speak. She could feel his breath against her skin like tiny puffs of air and it was like a sensuous caress, one that she wanted to go on. But she couldn't do this. Spencer Davis could very well have been involved with her sister and any attraction that she might feel was wrong until they found out the results of the paternity test.

On the one hand, she wanted Zoe to have a father, but on the other, she was hoping the test would be wrong. She was hoping Spencer Davis wasn't the type of man to knock up her sister and not even realize he had a child.

"Don't try and put the moves on me, Spencer Davis," Raina said, stepping away from him. "I told you before that I'm not interested."

Spencer raised an eyebrow as if he didn't believe her. "All right." He held up his hands. "But this isn't over between us. The test will show you you're wrong and I'm not the father. But just in case I'm wrong—know this, Raina Martin. If Zoe is my daughter, I will be seeking full custody."

Raina's mouth dropped open in shock just as Zoe came flying through the kitchen door with Raina's mother following right behind her.

Spencer backed away from Raina. He knew she was as attracted to him as he was to her. He'd felt it, sensed it, but now wasn't the right time to make his move. There was too much unresolved conflict between them. But once the test results showed he wasn't Zoe's father, he would have a chance to find out exactly what it was about Raina Martin that intrigued him so.

As the young girl came through the kitchen doors, Spencer looked at her closely. Memories of the night he'd met Alexa Martin came flooding back. And he knew who Zoe's father was: his brother.

Spencer bent low to the ground until he was the little girl's size so he wouldn't scare her with his height. He peered at her, memorizing all her features. She was Cameron's spitting image; she had his same nose, chin and big brown eyes. She was his niece. "Hi, Zoe."

Zoe looked at Spencer and then at Raina as if to ask, "Who is this?"

Spencer assumed the older woman was Raina's mother. She looked at her daughter questioningly. He figured she wanted to know who this strange man was who was speaking to Zoe.

"Zoe, this is...uh...my friend...Mr. Spencer," Raina offered, tripping over her words. He was sure she didn't know what to call him. She couldn't very well tell Zoe he could potentially be her father.

"Mr. Spencer, I'd also like to introduce you to my mother, Mrs. Martin." Raina's mother raised an eyebrow. Clearly, she recognized his name and knew who he was, but she remained silent when Spencer nodded his head in greeting.

"Zoe, say hello," Raina said in an attempt to break the awkward silence.

"You can just call me Spence," Spencer said to Zoe. "Can you do that?"

Zoe nodded and smiled. "Hi, Spence. It's nice to meet you." She offered her tiny hand to him, which he shook gently. "How do you know my auntie Raina?"

Spencer looked up at Raina and smiled. "We go way back." *All of three days.* "And it's nice to meet you, too. Did you just get off from school?"

"Yes," Zoe said and began rambling on about her day at school as if she'd known him for years. Clearly she had no fear of strangers and was quite friendly and sociable. He remembered Alexa was the same way.

Spencer humored Zoe and sat down with her after Raina had consented to milk and cookies for an after-school snack. They sat down at the small pedestal table in the back of the kitchen while Raina and her mother watched them from across the room.

"You're awfully tall. How tall are you?" Zoe inquired, noticing how uncomfortable it was for him to sit in an average chair.

"I'm six foot four."

"Are you a giant?" Zoe asked, dunking her cookie in the milk. "Like in the fairy tales?"

Spencer laughed heartily as he followed suit and dunked his cookie, too. "Sometimes it feels like that," he answered honestly. Especially in the sixth grade, when he'd skyrocketed above all the other boys in his class. It had gotten better once he'd gone to high school. When he'd joined the basketball team, he'd finally found a place where he fit in.

"Did it make you sad to be different?" Zoe inquired.

Spencer was surprised by the thoughtful question from the six-year-old. What was the saying? *Out of the mouths of babes...* "It used to, but not anymore."

"Zoe, stop questioning the man." Raina came forward to break up the moment he was having with Zoe to stand directly behind him. Spencer got the vibe that it was time for him to leave and then Raina confirmed it. "Plus I think Mr. Spencer has to go, don't you?"

Spencer turned around to look at Raina. Clearly she didn't like the bond he was forging with Zoe. But why? She was the one who'd started down this road. He would have thought she would be encouraging it, especially since she thought he was Zoe's father.

"Yes, I guess so." He rose awkwardly from the small table to stand over the little girl and Raina. "Princess Zoe." He reached for her hand, kissed it and bowed with a flourish. "I look forward to getting to know you better."

Zoe chuckled at his grandness and said, "You're funny, Spence."

"Goodbye, Zoe." Spencer turned on his heel to go. "A word, Raina?"

She must have heard the commanding tone in his voice because she followed him into the retail area of their catering shop.

"Yes?" Raina snapped, her arms folded across her chest.

Spencer was irritated by her hostile behavior. "You started this, Raina. Don't be upset with me because I'm running with it," he responded. "I'm trying to get to know the little girl *you* claim is my daughter, so a little less acrimony would be good here."

His response knocked some of the wind out of her sails and Raina unfolded her arms and her shoulders relaxed. She blinked several times and said, "I'm sorry. It's just that Zoe responded to you like she'd known you for years and with me..." Her voice trailed off.

"Of course she's going to be harder on you," Spencer said, softening his voice. "You're in the trenches day in and day out. You're the one she's going to take out all her hurt and loss on."

Raina looked up at him as if she was surprised that he could understand what she'd been going through. *But isn't that what she is looking for, someone to take the load off her with Zoe?*

"It's been hard on her, losing Alexa so young," Raina supplied. "I'm doing my best, but it's not easy."

"Of course it's difficult. Zoe may have lost her

mother, but you lost your sister, *your twin*. That must
be harder than any of the rest of us can imagine."

Raina swallowed, and he could see her biting back
her tears. He hadn't wanted her to cry. He'd only wanted
her to know that he understood and could be there. If
she wanted.

"Thank you." Raina nodded. "I think everyone
seems to forget that I lost Alexa, too."

Spencer reached across and caressed Raina's cheek.
"I understand loss." He was still dealing with the ramifications of losing Cameron four years later. He could
only imagine how much worse it would be if he'd had
to contend with rearing a child after such a loss.

Raina looked up as if to ask him a question, but
Spencer felt it was time to leave. He swiftly moved
toward the door. "I'll be in touch about the timing of
the test. As both our attorneys stated, it'll better if the
test is done at an independent laboratory to avoid any
conflict."

Seconds later, Spencer was out the door and breathing a sigh of release. Raina Martin was quickly getting
under his skin. He'd wanted to comfort her and take
away the pain he knew she was feeling by spilling his
guts about the loss of his brother. But he had no right to
put that on Raina; it was his cross to bear and his alone.

Raina stared at the door Spencer had just departed
out of. He'd been surprisingly comforting when he'd
told her that she was suffering as much as Zoe. It was
as if he'd looked deep inside her soul and read her mind.
And it scared her.

When he'd said he knew loss, she knew it wasn't a
line. He wasn't using it as way to get into her panties

though she had no doubt that's exactly what Spencer wanted to do. She'd known it from the moment she'd laid eyes on him at the fund-raising dinner. The fact that he'd personally come to see her today even after finding out that she'd served him with paternity papers confirmed it. Spencer Davis wanted her. The question was did she want him? And if she did, would she act on it?

"Raina." Her mother called her name from the doorway of the kitchen. "Was that who I think it was?" she asked, coming into the retail store.

"Yes," Raina replied, moving away from the door and walking behind the counter to find a rag to wipe off the counter. She needed to do something to try to avoid the conversation she knew her mother wanted to have. No such luck; her mother went in for the kill.

"What does he want?"

"I don't know, Mom," Raina replied, shrugging her shoulders as she wiped the counter.

"Don't give me a pat answer, Raina Martin." Crystal grabbed her by the shoulders and stopped her from working. "More importantly I want to know what was going on between you two."

"What do you mean?" Raina asked innocently.

"Body language," her mother offered. "That man was clearly interested in you. What kind of man would hit on the woman raising his daughter? It's deplorable."

"We don't know Spencer is Zoe's father," Raina said, surprising herself by coming to Spencer's defense and jerking her shoulders away.

"But Alexa said that Spencer was the one."

"No, what she said was Spencer could help." Raina remembered her sister's last words very carefully because she'd replayed them in her head a million times.

And since meeting Spencer, she was finding it hard to believe that in this day and age he would be so careless as to expose himself to diseases, much less pregnancy, by not practicing safe sex. Spencer struck her as a smart man.

"Yeah, well, I think it's him. Why else would Alexa have carried that picture with her all these years?"

"Perhaps as a clue to find the real father."

"Why are you grasping at straws here?" Her mother looked at her. "This was your idea. I thought you wanted to find Zoe's father. If it had been up to your father and I, we would have let the matter rest and raised Zoe ourselves."

"Well, it's not up to you," Raina snapped. She was aware that her parents thought her inept at the parenting thing, but Alexa had chosen her. "I'm Zoe's guardian, and she confided in me how she wished she was like other kids with two parents. If you'd heard her and how upset she was, you would know that's what I'm trying to give her."

"I just hope your good intentions don't come back and smack you in the face." Crystal seemed unfazed by Raina's harsh tone. "Because if he is Zoe's father, he has rights, too, you know."

Raina rolled her eyes. She already knew this. Spencer had made it painfully clear that should he be deemed the father, he would sue her for full custody. But Raina thought it was a bluff. What thirty-eight-year-old man wanted to be a single parent to a six-year-old little girl? Although he'd had a way with Zoe earlier, she highly doubted Spencer had been around children often, much less knew how to raise one. *It's not like you do, either,* her inner voice mocked.

"All right, Mom." Raina threw up her hands in resignation. "We're never going to see eye to eye on my decision to find Zoe's biological father, so let's just get ready for dinner."

Spencer stared out at the Miami shoreline from the balcony of the bedroom in his penthouse. The sky was dark without a star to be seen. It was kind of how he felt at the realization of knowing exactly who Zoe was. Seeing the child in person had told him everything he needed to know. He wasn't the father, and the paternity test he'd agreed to take would show that, but his brother made Zoe family.

Spencer recalled the night he and Cameron had met Alexa Martin. She'd come on strong, hanging outside the arena with several of her groupie friends. They all had perfectly done hair, nails and makeup. She'd been wearing one of those skimpy minidresses that showed off every God-given curve. Initially Spencer had shown interest in her, thus the photograph. But once Cameron had seen her later that evening at the club, he'd been smitten. As the evening wore on, his brother's special charm had literally dazzled the clothes right off Alexa.

Spencer hadn't been upset because he and his brother had vowed never to let a woman come between them. And so Cameron and Alexa had begun a torrid love affair for several weeks, right under Cameron's wife's nose. Spencer had warned him that it wouldn't end well, and it hadn't. News of another of Cameron's affairs had hit the papers and his face was splashed all over the news. He'd immediately called it quits, much to Alexa's consternation.

Now that Spencer thought about it, Alexa had called

him once, several weeks after they'd broken up, asking for Cameron's new phone number. Spencer had advised Alexa to give up the ghost. His brother was not the commitment kind. Had she been trying to tell Cameron she was pregnant back then? Had Spencer gotten in the way? Spencer had been trying to help by saving her from embarrassment, hurt and anger, but was he to blame for Cameron never finding out he'd sired a child?

Spencer felt terrible. Perhaps knowing that he'd had a child would have cured Cameron of all his bad behavior. Was that why in her final hour, Alexa had told Raina that he would help her? Because he was Zoe's uncle? She probably thought he would be able to given that Cameron had passed away. His death had been publicized in all the Miami papers and Alexa had to have known the truth.

It was incumbent on Spencer to do right by his niece this time. He realized what he had to do. He would have to run a separate DNA test to confirm Cameron was the father and then Zoe would be entitled to Cameron's estate and a whole lot more.

Chapter 4

Raina sat in the uncomfortable steel chair in the laboratory waiting room, wringing her hands as she waited for the nurse to call her and Zoe in. She felt terrible because she'd lied to Zoe. She'd told her that they had to take some medical test for school. She hadn't known what else to say. She wasn't ready to have the conversation with Zoe about who Spencer could be until she was sure of their connection.

And they would find out soon enough. She'd called the day before to find out exactly how long the test would take and they'd indicated they would have the results in a few days. She'd thought it would take weeks like she'd seen on television, but technology had come a long way. Rather than take blood, all they had to do was swab Zoe's cheek for DNA and compare it to Spencer's and they would know the truth.

The knowledge didn't make feel Raina feel any better. On the one hand, if Spencer wasn't Zoe's father, then it was back to the drawing board to figure out who Alexa could have possibly slept with. The news would be great for Spencer because he would have no obligation to her or Zoe and could move on with his life. Or would he? Perhaps he was looking to bed Raina to see if she would succumb to his charms like most women did.

Then there was the other hand they could be dealt. Spencer could indeed be Zoe's father and then all hell was going to break loose. Raina would have to explain to Zoe exactly who he was and why he hadn't been a part of her life for the past six years. *How did you even explain something like that to a child?* Then she and Spencer would have to come up with some type of custody arrangement. Or worse yet, he would try and sue her for custody and their relationship could get ugly, real quick.

If she was honest with herself, Raina didn't relish the latter prospect. Although she knew it would be good for Zoe to have a father and two parents, deep down she was secretly hoping that Spencer was right and he wasn't the father. Because then…then…she could what? Give in to the fantasies she'd been having about the sexy former basketball star?

"Good morning," a deep voice said from above her, jostling Raina out of her thoughts. "How are my two girls this morning?" Spencer asked, peering down at her.

Raina swallowed. Spencer looked even sexier today. He was wearing a pullover sweater, worn jeans and gleaming new tennis shoes. "Good morning," she managed to say after several interminable moments.

Spencer removed his hands from behind his back and produced two cups. "Hot chocolate for my lady." He handed Zoe the smaller cup. "Coffee for you, my dear." He handed the other to Raina.

Yet again, she was surprised by his thoughtfulness. Surely this man couldn't be someone who'd bedded her sister, gotten her pregnant and then turned his back on her without a second glance. "Thank you," she murmured. She needed a dose of caffeine to snap her awake and make her realize that she didn't really *know* Spencer Davis. He could be that man, even though her gut hoped he wasn't.

"You're welcome," he said, sliding easily into the chair next to her.

"What are you doing here, Spence?" Zoe inquired as she sipped on her hot chocolate.

Raina turned to her niece. *Smart girl.* She came up with a plausible excuse. "Mr. Spencer thought we might want company or that you might be scared."

Zoe made a funny face and then turned to her accusingly. "I thought you said there would be no needles."

"There won't be."

"Then I'll be okay. I'm not a baby, Auntie Raina," Zoe admonished.

Spencer gave Raina a sideways glance and whispered, "I guess she told you."

"Yeah, she can be a little too smart," Raina murmured back, then turned to Zoe. "I know that. Did you ever think Auntie Raina might want the company and want to spend time with a friend?"

The second the sentence was out of her mouth, Raina realized just how true that statement was. Having someone like Spencer interested in her had certainly piqued her female sensibilities. And she could see Spencer smiling from beside her. Clearly he'd liked her response, too.

"Yes, I'm just here to keep your auntie company." Spencer eyed Raina and gave her a wink. "And then I thought perhaps later after the test we could go to the Harvest Festival in Coconut Grove by Biscayne Bay when we're done."

"Festival?" Raina asked.

"I thought it might be fun," Spencer said nonchalantly. "That is, if you don't have any other plans?"

"We never have any plans," Zoe answered for Raina. "Auntie Raina works all the time and then we go home and watch TV."

Raina closed her eyes and prayed for sanity. She wished her niece would not be so honest. She didn't want Spencer to know she was a workaholic who couldn't remember her last date. But then, what did she want?

"Ms. Martin, we are ready for you and your niece," a technician said from the doorway.

"See you soon." Spencer waved as Raina and Zoe rose from their chairs.

"You'll be here when we get back, Spence?" Zoe inquired, a note of hope in her tiny little voice.

"Yes, ma'am," he replied, beaming at her.

Raina stopped at the doorway and smiled at Spencer. She mouthed the words "Thank you" right before she walked through the door.

Twenty minutes later, they'd all reconvened in the lobby. They'd come for Spencer seconds after Zoe and he'd taken his test. After producing a court order drafted by his attorney, he'd also requested a second test be run against his brother Cameron's DNA, which had been kept on file by another medical lab.

Cameron's attorney had been shocked when Spencer had told him that he suspected Cameron was Zoe's father. They'd discussed the ramifications if the test revealed the truth. Thanks to a paternity pickle a few years back, Cameron had added a clause in his will about future heirs. If anything should happen to him, he named Spencer as guardian. The attorney had informed Spencer that he potentially had as much right to custody of Zoe as Raina or her family.

Spencer wasn't sure how he felt about suing for custody or even shared custody; he just knew that he wanted a place in Zoe's life. And in a few days, Raina would know he wasn't the scoundrel who'd bedded her sister. Then they could finally act on what was going on between them. And there was definitely something going on. Just sitting next to Raina, he'd felt an electrical charge going back and forth between them even though only their shoulders touched.

But he also knew Raina wouldn't get involved with him if she thought he'd been with Alexa. So he was going to have to show a little patience until the test results came in.

"How did everything go?" Spencer asked his niece. It was so amazing that although Cameron had died, a part of him still lived on.

"It was easy," Zoe said. "Not like before with all the needles. They just swabbed my cheek."

"You're a brave girl," Spencer said, looking at Raina. "And I think brave little girls deserve some fun at the Harvest Festival. What do you say, Auntie?" He wanted to spend some more time getting to know his niece and the added bonus was the time he'd spend with Raina.

Raina stared daggers at Spencer. He'd baited her into this situation so she would have no choice but to agree otherwise Zoe would be upset. "Uh, sure, we can spend a few hours."

"Excellent. C'mon, Zoe." Spencer grabbed the little girl's hand and placed his other on the small of Raina's back and led her out of the laboratory.

They decided to leave Raina's car at the lab and come back for it later. After Spencer helped Raina into the passenger side and Zoe into the backseat of his Bentley, he came around to the driver side. The car was a lot less ostentatious than Raina had expected. She'd expected that every athlete had a Ferrari or Lamborghini, but this car was luxurious and practical.

"What is a Harvest Festival?" Zoe asked from the backseat.

"Well, Zoe, it's a festival where we celebrate the local farmers, gardeners and nonprofit organizations. We can buy fresh produce, vegetables and meat from local farmers. You can see all the gardens that the schools, churches and organizations have planted and play games and make crafts. And best of all, we'll get to taste the delicious farm-fresh food from the food trucks."

"That sounds like fun."

"There will be lots of seminars, workshops and roundtables focused on our local food system. And, Raina, you'll love this—they've got cooking demonstrations and organic gardening sessions. You might take away a few things for your catering business."

"That's our philosophy at Diamonds and Gems Catering. Summer and I try to use locally grown and organic ingredients when we can. People don't realize how many chemicals are in our food. I make sure Zoe and I eat as many organic vegetables as possible."

"I hate veggies," Zoe said.

"You have to eat them," Spencer said. "How else do you think you'll grow up to be big and strong, like your auntie Raina?" Spencer gave Raina a cursory glance before turning his attention back to the road. "I heard they've got some great bluegrass, traditional and local bands playing."

"I'm not big on folk music," Raina replied. "But I'm game for everything else."

Spencer drove to Coconut Grove and parked in a private lot across from the festival. The fall foliage and rustic decor made the grounds look festive. They walked around the venue, taking in the sights and sounds.

Spencer was knowledgeable and talked to Raina about farming and organic foods. He stopped to show Zoe a special garden. When he grabbed Raina's hand and led her to one of the food trucks to sample a local dish, Raina didn't remove her hand.

Instead she allowed him to lead and didn't object when he paid for the meal. "Thank you," she said when he handed her a small paper plate. "What is it?"

"A Baja fish taco," Spencer replied. "Made with local mahi-mahi. Would you like to taste it, Zoe?" he asked, looking down at his niece.

Zoe glanced up at him with her doelike eyes and said, "No, but can I have a hot dog?"

"A hot dog?" Spencer frowned. He couldn't remember the last time he'd had one of those, but children seemed to love them. "Sure thing, kiddo. We'll find you a hot dog." He and Raina walked down the rows of vendors, eating their fish tacos and searching for a hot dog.

When Raina paused to check out some avocados, he noticed she had sauce on the side of her face. He reached across and wiped it off with his thumb. Unconsciously, he licked it off his hand and he watched Raina's café au lait skin flush from the intimacy of his action. Their eyes connected in that moment and Spencer could swear Raina wanted him to kiss her. He would have liked nothing better, but now wasn't the right moment for that.

"There's a hot dog vendor," Spencer said, breaking the moment between them. A few minutes later, he was handing a purveyor a five-dollar bill and handing Zoe a hot dog covered with mustard and ketchup.

"And what do you say?" Raina said, looking down at Zoe.

"Thank you, Spence."

"You're welcome, Zoe."

They enjoyed the day as if they were a family enjoying a Saturday outing. Spencer had never realized he'd wanted a family until that moment. Spending time with Raina and Zoe was showing him he wanted a family of his own. And he could possibly have this one.

Raina stopped to watch a collard greens cooking presentation while Spencer went off with Zoe to get her face painted. It gave Raina time alone to collect her thoughts and her emotions. Spencer had been the perfect companion, making Raina realize just how much she missed having a man in her life. And no matter what the test results showed, Raina resolved to make time for herself and a relationship a priority.

When they returned, Raina had picked up several autumn vegetables like collards, sweet potatoes and cauliflower along with various selections of meats, cheeses, breads and a scrumptious homemade apple pie from a local farmer.

Spencer eyed the haul Raina had acquired while he and Zoe had been busy. "Will you be making dinner for us later?"

"Why? Were you looking for an invite?" Raina asked, smiling.

"And if I was?"

While Zoe asked one of the vendors about his plants, Raina pulled Spencer aside. "I appreciate all the flirting, but you know this can't work."

"I don't know what you mean."

"Yes, you do," Raina said. "This, you and me." She pointed back and forth between the two of them.

"Because we don't know the results?" he offered. "Well, we'll know soon enough. Can't we just let sleeping dogs lie and enjoy each other's company?"

Raina tried to protest, but Spencer put his index finger on her lips. "Just for today. I'm having a lot of fun with you and Zoe, and I'd like it to continue. Is that so bad?"

Raina pursed her lips. It wasn't bad. And she was having fun herself, too much fun, which was why she wanted to put some distance between her and Spencer. He was quite the charmer and he seemed to have a way with Zoe. She hadn't seen her niece this happy, well, since before Alexa had passed. Sure, she'd been to a birthday party here and there, but Raina had watched Zoe and knew that she was putting on a show, acting happy because that's what all the adults in her life expected. But Raina knew otherwise. She was there every night when Zoe would cry softly into her pillow because she missed her mother terribly.

"Okay, okay," Raina relented. She didn't want to fight with Spencer, and it was nice having the company.

It was dusk by the time they headed back to the car to put Raina's groceries in the trunk. Zoe exclaimed, "We can't go! We haven't been on a hayride yet."

"Zoe, it's late, and we should head back so I can make dinner."

"Spence." Zoe looked at Spencer with pleading eyes to convince her aunt to stay.

It seemed her plea tugged at Spencer's heartstrings, and he looked at Raina. "I know you have food in the car, but it's cool out and it's only a half-hour ride. What do you say?"

Raina rolled her eyes. Spencer was spoiling her niece. Whatever she'd asked for, from hot dogs to cotton candy to stuffed animals, he'd been unable to resist her. Raina had found it endearing that Zoe had him wrapped around her little finger, but she also knew she would pay for it later when Zoe was hyper and wouldn't go to bed.

"Okay, one ride," Raina replied.

A farmer helped them climb into a two-horse wagon filled with hay. A few moments later a family of four joined them, and soon they were trotting down the festival road.

"This is so fun," Zoe said excitedly and then she promptly climbed up near the farmer in the front of the wagon and started asking him questions. Raina watched as the farmer allowed her to hold one of the reins while keeping his hand on the other.

"She's adorable," Spencer said from Raina's side, and she turned to look up at him.

"Yeah, she is pretty special." She watched him slide down farther in the hay and then open his arms to her.

"I promise I won't bite," Spencer said.

Raina debated with herself on whether she wanted to snuggle with him on the hayride. She threw caution to the wind and leaned back into his embrace.

Spencer's arms settled around her, and Raina allowed herself to be comforted by him. She could feel the hard expanse of his chiseled chest behind her even with all her clothes on. And his arms, well they were rock solid and held her with ease. When Spencer tugged her ever so slightly to face him, Raina saw the sexy gleam lurking in his dark brown eyes. She knew she should resist what she knew was about to happen, but she didn't.

Spencer's lifted his head toward her and he brushed his lips briefly but firmly across hers. His lips were featherlight yet determined as they caressed hers, and a soft sigh escaped her. He threaded his fingers through her wavy curls and her lips parted of their own accord. His tongue slipped inside her warm and waiting mouth and explored the recesses, filling, learning and savoring every inch of her. He devoured her with his seductive kiss in such a possessive and primitive way that it left Raina wanting more.

Raina had to force herself to push Spencer away, her lips still tingling from his kiss. His heat and breath against her face overwhelmed her.

What the hell was she doing? Spencer could have been with Alexa! She'd gotten caught up in the moment and allowed herself to let go, and look what had happened. He'd been seducing her all day with his charms and she'd fallen prey to them like an innocent school-girl. "That kiss should have never happened."

"I disagree," he whispered. "That kiss has been in the making since the moment I laid eyes on you. I've wanted to know if you would taste as sweet as you looked, and you didn't disappoint."

Raina's breath hitched in her throat. He'd rendered her speechless. She could hear her heart pounding in her chest, and her pulse had quickened.

"Auntie Raina." Zoe jumped back down to join them, startling them both.

Raina looked at Spencer guiltily, but neither of them said a word. "Did you see me, Auntie? I was steering the horses."

"Yes, babydoll, you did a good job," Raina replied, finally finding her voice. "And it's time for us to get off."

As soon as the wagon came to a complete stop, Raina was scrambling down the steps the farmer had erected to help them off.

Raina was quiet on the ride back to her car at the laboratory, but Zoe filled the silence by chatting about how much fun she'd had, what she'd eaten, what she'd bought and what she'd made.

Spencer meanwhile was gripping the steering wheel. He only spoke when he exited to help Zoe out of the car.

"So you had fun today?" he asked, bending down to her height.

"I did. Thank you, Spence." Zoe leaned over to give Spencer a hug and Raina felt deep in her stomach just how heartfelt it was.

Once Raina had safely ensconced Zoe in the back-seat, she turned around to face Spencer. "Well thank you for a lovely outing. You can retire now from playing daddy."

"Excuse me?" Spencer asked.

"You're off the hook. You did a great job playing devoted father, but you don't have to try so hard to seduce me. Clearly, you think I must be as easy as my sister." Raina didn't know why she was being so spiteful. Was she purposely trying to bait him into a fight? She must have angered him because his eyes blazed fire.

"You think that that's what today was all about?" Spencer inquired. "Getting you into bed?" He laughed derisively and pulled out his cell phone. "All I have to do is call any number of willing females and they'd be all too happy to spend time in my company. I don't *need* to hang out with an uptight workaholic caterer to get my jollies."

Raina was stunned by his harsh words. She recovered to say, "Well, then, let me rid you of my deplorable company." She reached for the driver's door handle, but Spencer pushed the door closed.

"Raina." Spencer sighed heavily. "Let's not ruin a perfectly good day. I'm sorry if you feel I crossed the line with you earlier. I won't apologize for kissing you, but perhaps I moved too fast. I just feel that there's something between us." He reached to grab her, but Raina was quicker and rushed inside the vehicle.

She locked the door but rolled down the window. "I'll be in touch," she said. Seconds later, she was pulling out of the space and leaving a stunned Spencer standing in the parking lot, staring after her.

Chapter 5

"You didn't call me this weekend," Summer said when Raina came into work on Monday morning carrying several recyclable grocery bags. "How did everything go at the laboratory on Saturday?"

"Fine," Raina answered, wrapping her apron around her middle. She unpacked the delicacies she'd found at the festival and put them away in the cupboard and refrigerator.

She'd slept fitfully the past two nights after her kiss with Spencer. She felt guilty as hell for losing control and acting on her feelings. But it had been hard not to when he was being all charming and gallant, catering to her and Zoe's every need. Spencer had shown her what her life could look like if he was a part of it, and she'd liked it.

"Don't 'fine' me, Raina Martin," Summer said, grabbing Raina by the shoulders and forcing her to look at her. "Are you holding out on me? What happened?"

"I'm not holding out," Raina said, averting her eyes so she didn't have to look at her best friend. Summer could always read her and knew when she was lying about something.

"Yes, you are," Summer said. "Did something happen at the lab?"

Raina sighed heavily. Summer wasn't going to give up pressuring her for answers, so she had better just get the Spanish Inquisition over. "Spencer met us at the lab."

"Ah!" Summer released her shoulders. "And?"

"And he brought coffee and hot chocolate for me and Zoe."

"I know there's more, Raina, so you might as well just spit it out."

"Then he invited us to the Coconut Grove Harvest Festival."

"Really? I wanted to attend, but I couldn't convince Ryan to come with me. Since we'd been working a few late nights, he'd missed me and wanted me all to himself this weekend. We barely came up for air."

Raina smiled. Ryan Tucker was Summer's live-in boyfriend. They'd been together since high school. They knew everything about each other and could finish each other's sentences. Raina had always envied their enduring relationship. "Well you missed some great locally grown food, I brought some cheeses and pâtés that we can use for our next party."

"That's work, and that's all fine and good, but why don't we get back to your date with Spencer?"

Raina flushed bright red. "It wasn't a date."

Summer raised a brow. "Wasn't it?"

"No, it wasn't." Raina shook her head furiously, more to convince herself than Summer. "We simply took Zoe out for a day on the town. She was able to make crafts and play games…" Her words trailed off and she went over to the sink to wash her hands.

"So, this was all about Zoe?" Summer asked and then chuckled at her question. "Who are you trying to fool, Raina? Me? Or yourself? It was most definitely a date whether your niece accompanied you or not. Spencer Davis was dying to take you out and he found a way to accomplish it without scaring you off."

"Well, he did that when he kissed me." She dried off her hands with the towel hanging on the wall rack.

Her sentence momentarily shocked Summer into silence.

"Did you hear me?" Raina asked. "I said he kissed me."

Summer blinked several times before inquiring, "Well, did you kiss him back?"

Raina rolled her eyes. "I didn't have much choice. He kind of took over the situation, convincing me to respond to him. It was all very disconcerting."

Summer watched Raina and noticed how her eyes grew wistful. "Sounds great if you ask me." She gave a hoot when Raina swatted her with the towel.

"And it was," Raina admitted. "And that's the problem, Summer. You know I can't get involved with Spencer. He was involved with my sister, possibly fathered her child."

"Yeah, well, forgive me, but your sister is gone and you're still here. And you'll know soon enough if Spencer's the father. Until then, you shouldn't wind yourself in circles over this. You don't know anything yet. There was no harm in kissing a sexy, attractive, available man."

"No, but Zoe needs a father," Raina said. "It isn't fair that I put my needs above hers."

"And you need a man," Summer replied and then held up her palm in defense because she knew Raina was about to go into attack mode. "And I don't mean in a needy way, but like me and Ryan, you need someone to complement you. Spencer Davis could be that person. You're entitled to some happiness, Raina."

"I know that."

"Do you?" Summer asked. "Because you've been so worried about being there for Zoe and comforting your parents that you've overlooked yourself and your own needs."

"I'm all they have left."

"I know they all adored Alexa, but you're not the consolation prize."

Raina stared at Summer. "I know that."

"Do you really? Because I've always thought you were amazing, Raina Martin. You just need to know it. So how did you leave things with Spencer?"

Raina frowned. "Not good. I accused him of trying to play daddy. I told him the role didn't suit him and he shouldn't try so hard to get into my panties."

"Ouch!"

"I know it was harsh, but I had to push him away until I know the truth. Otherwise he'd keep coming on strong."

"When will you know the results?"

"Before the end of the week. It can't be soon enough."

* * *

Spencer stared down at the piece of paper showing the test results. It had been couriered over to him earlier that morning. The first set against him and Zoe showed what he already knew: he wasn't Zoe's father. The second test also proved exactly what he'd thought; his brother was Zoe's father.

The paper slipped out of Spencer's hand and fell onto the mahogany desk. Cameron would never know he'd fathered a beautiful little girl like Zoe Martin. She was bright and funny just like Cameron, but he would never get the chance to see her first recital, help her drive her first car, watch her go to her prom or walk her down the aisle. All those moments had been stolen because of the accident.

Spencer shook his head. Now it was up to him to do right by Cameron's child. He had Cameron's full power of attorney and therefore was legally responsible for her and her inheritance. He was thinking about how he was going to set up a trust for Zoe when Raina came bursting through the door of his office, holding the results in her hand.

The look on her face told him that she'd seen the results and knew he wasn't Zoe's father. He would have thought she would be happier, but she looked devastated.

"So, you're not the father," Raina said, running her fingers through her black hair, which hung in long tumultuous waves down her back. He'd never seen her hair in its natural state. It was wild, unruly and completely sexy.

"I'm sorry, Mr. Davis." Mona was standing behind Raina. "She just barged in."

Spencer held up his hand. "It's okay, Mona. I can take it from here."

After eyeing Raina suspiciously, Mona reluctantly closed the door behind her.

"Would you like a glass of water?" Spencer asked, rising from his seat to go toward his wet bar. He grasped a tumbler and opened a bottle of water and poured the liquid inside.

"I don't need any water," Raina spat as she glared at him from the doorway. "I don't understand these results. I was almost certain you were the father."

"I think you should come and sit." Spencer motioned to the plush leather sofa.

"I'd rather stand," Raina said, as if she was afraid to come near him.

"Fine, have it your way," he said, unbuttoning his suit jacket and sitting down on the sofa. She was as stubborn as a mule and could stand while he told his story, Cameron's story. He sipped on the water he'd poured for her.

"You knew my sister and the timing was all right." Raina shook her head. "I don't understand. It all made sense."

"Well, I for one am happy about the results," Spencer replied.

"I just bet," Raina responded,. "Now you don't have to worry about me coming after you for child support. And you don't have to worry about playing daddy because Zoe's not yours. You can move on with your life."

"It's not that simple," Spencer said, sitting up. "I was never concerned about supporting Zoe if she was my child. I am more than capable of taking care of her."

"Then what did you mean?" Raina asked. She stopped as she walked toward him. "Wait a minute.

If you're not Zoe's father, then you know who is." She was starting to put the pieces together. "There was a reason my sister told me to come to you for help. You know something. What is it?" Her eyes pierced his, demanding the truth.

"Yes. I know who Zoe's father is," Spencer acknowledged.

"Then why did you put me, put Zoe, through this?"

"Because you were so absolutely sure you were right that for a second I started to doubt myself. My recollections of that time period are a bit hazy." He paused. "All the drinking and partying. I wondered if there was any truth to what you were saying."

"Okay, that's plausible," Raina said as if mulling over her words. "But you figured this out before the test came in, didn't you?"

Spencer was surprised by her quick perception. "Yes, I recalled that Alexa was seeing my brother during that time."

"And you think he's the father?" She began pacing the floor. Then she turned back to Spencer. "Why?"

"Cameron met Alexa the same night I did. The same night that photograph of us was taken. They had a hot and heavy affair that lasted over a month. It fizzled when Cameron got caught cheating on his wife with another woman other than your sister."

"But that doesn't mean he's the father," Raina countered. "We shouldn't leap to conclusions like I did with you."

"I'm not speculating," Spencer said. "I'm certain."

She peered at him with those almond-shaped eyes. "How can you be so sure?"

Spencer sighed. "Because I ran a second paternity test at the laboratory in conjunction with ours."

"You did what?" Her voice rose several octaves.

Spencer stood and leaned over his desk so he could produce the second set of paternity results. "I wanted to be one hundred percent sure before I raised your hopes again. And I am now." He handed Raina the results.

Raina's eyes quickly darted over the test. When they came into contact with his again, they blazed with anger. "And why would you keep something like this to yourself?" she demanded. "Was this just a way to get closer to me? You had no right to keep this information from me."

Spencer reached for her shoulders. "Calm down, Raina."

"I won't calm down." She stepped away from him. She seemed to be getting more and more distraught as the minutes ticked by. "I'm trying to give Zoe a father and instead you lie and manipulate me into spending time with you."

"I never lied to you," Spencer replied harshly. "I didn't realize the truth."

"But when you did, you kept it to yourself. And now...and now..."

Spencer saw the moment reality hit Raina and she remembered that Cameron had died in a car crash four years earlier. Horror crossed her face and she stepped backward, stumbling until she reached the sofa, her hand clutching her mouth. "Ohmigod!"

Spencer instantly rushed over to the couch to comfort her. She looked up at him, tears glistening in her eyes. "Dear God!" Raina cried. "Zoe hasn't just lost her mother. She's lost her father, too!" Raina held her stomach as sobs began to rack her entire body.

Spencer's arms came around Raina's slender frame. "It's okay," he soothed her. He allowed her to cry onto his suit, stroking her hair and back until she began to quiet.

Some time later, Raina eventually got a hold of herself and her emotions. She was trying to sort out everything Spencer had just told her and the ramifications of it all. She was it. Raina and her parents were all the family Zoe had left because she was an orphan. Her mother had died of cervical cancer and her father in a car crash.

Raina recalled the news reports and seeing photos of the crumpled car on television and in newspapers. Spencer and Cameron had been considered basketball royalty. Cameron's passing had caused quite a debate about seat belt laws. If she remembered correctly, he hadn't been wearing one, but Spencer had and he'd survived. And wait…now he too was Zoe's family. He was her uncle.

Eventually Raina slid from the comfort of Spencer's arms to stare at him. "I'm sorry," she said humbly. She'd accused him of keeping the truth from her, but as he'd said his memories of back then were a bit fuzzy.

"For what?" Spencer said.

"I said some pretty nasty things."

"Yeah, well, you were in shock," Spencer said. "You expected the results to say I was the father, but I'm not. Cameron is."

"And Zoe still doesn't get a father."

Spencer nodded. "True, but she's entitled to Cameron's legacy and, as trustee of his will, I can see to that."

Raina sighed. "It was never about the money, Spencer."

"I know that, but at least it'll help pay for her upbringing, her college education, maybe even her wedding one day."

Raina began to tear up as she nodded. "But it won't bring her father back."

Spencer touched Raina's thigh and she nearly jumped off the couch at the spark she felt. "I know, but I'll do everything I can for Zoe."

"*You* don't owe us anything," Raina said, slowly rising from the couch and pulling her purse over her shoulder. She started toward the door, but Spencer rose and stood in her path.

"Please don't leave like this. I'd like to talk to you about the provisions of Cameron's will. There is a clause that talks about any potential heirs."

"Not now," Raina said. Fate had stepped in and made a clear path for her to stay away from Spencer as he was dangerous to her health.

"Don't deny Zoe what she's entitled to," Spencer said, "because you're afraid to spend time with me."

Raina spun around to face him. "I'm not afraid."

"No?" Spencer stalked purposely toward her with an intense sexual look in his eyes.

Raina was frozen and stood still as their gazes locked. He seemed to be measuring her next step and devising a plan. Would she stand or take flight? Her pulse was skyrocketing because she knew that at any moment his mouth would claim hers as he'd done on the hayride and she would run out of options, but she still didn't run.

"It would have been easier for you if I was Zoe's father because then you'd be justified at keeping me at arm's length. But now there's no reason why we can't see each other, and you're running scared."

Drawing a deep breath, Raina replied, "You're wrong. You're just upset that I'm turning you, the legendary Spencer Davis, down. Well all of us can't fall at your feet."

"You don't say." When he reached her, one arm circled around her waist and he pulled her closer to him. "Why don't we test your theory?"

He brushed his mouth slowly, excruciatingly across hers, barely grazing her bottom lip. She gasped and it gave Spencer a fraction of an opening to make her melt against him. And melt she did.

He sealed his mouth to hers and her body called her out on her lie. She was totally affected by him. Her entire being tingled from his kiss and when his teeth tugged on her bottom lip, she opened her mouth to him, and he took full advantage.

His warm tongue swept inside her mouth, searching for hers and lighting a fire deep within her belly. She'd never been kissed like this before, so thoroughly, so passionately that she held on to him for dear life. She gave a small sigh of pleasure and wound her arms around his neck, kissing him back.

Spencer groaned and his fingers dived into her hair as he brought his body colliding against hers, causing her nipples to strain underneath the plaid shirt she wore, aching with an unfulfilled sexual energy. She tipped her head back and he moved, bracing her against the wall. Her legs were between his rock hard thighs so he could align their bodies and she could feel him, hard and throbbing against her.

Somehow he found the strength to pull away, and when he did Raina was limp in his arms. "So dinner then?" Spencer asked, sucking in a ragged breath. He'd proven his point. She wasn't immune to him.

Mindlessly, Raina nodded her consent. She'd been deprived of male company for too long and she wanted the ache she'd been experiencing since she'd met Spencer to ease.

She wanted him.

Chapter 6

"**D**id I hear you correctly?" Summer inquired. "Did you just say you're going out with Spencer Davis? Willingly?"

"Yes," Raina said over the phone as she rubbed scented lotion on her skin after taking a long, hot shower. "And I know its short notice, but can you watch Zoe for me?"

"I thought you said you weren't interested in the man."

"I'm not. We're going out to discuss Zoe," Raina said.

"But Spencer isn't the father."

"No, but apparently his brother Cameron was and he's executor of his will."

"So, this is strictly business?" Summer asked.

"Exactly." Raina spritzed perfume on her palms, neck, behind her ears and between her breasts.

Summer laughed. "I don't believe that for a second. Why don't you admit you like the man and want to spend more time with him?"

Raina stopped getting ready. "If I do, will that get you off my back?"

"Maybe."

"Then, fine." Raina sighed. "I'm going out with Spencer because I enjoy his company."

"And you're attracted to him?"

Raina's mind spun back to the second kiss in Spencer's office, which had been even more seductive and intoxicating than the first on the hayride. "Yes."

"Then have Zoe bring an overnight bag," Summer said.

That snapped Raina out of her daydreaming. "No, no," she said, shaking her head fervently as if Summer could see her. "I don't intend on going to bed with Spencer. We're just sharing a meal together."

"Humph" was all she heard from the other end of the line and then the dial tone.

Raina clicked the end button on her cell phone. What was Summer thinking? She wasn't into casual sex, never had been. In fact, she could count her sexual partners on one hand. Not to mention the thought of going to bed with Spencer terrified her. Although he wasn't Wilt Chamberlain, she was sure Spencer had had his share of sexual conquests. Women lined up to go to bed with athletes and movie stars, and Raina had no desire to become one of them.

Yet her mind told her to wear the sexiest underwear in her repertoire. As she rummaged through her bureau, Raina realized she didn't have a lot to choose from. She was most comfortable in simple briefs. She wished she had more of a selection of lacy, satin nothings to choose from. She recalled a set she'd shoved into the back of the drawer from one of her and Summer's shopping sprees. It would have to do.

Raina slid the lace demi bra with mesh netting over her shoulders and pulled up the matching bikini panties. She did not intend the evening to end with Spencer getting a chance to see her in her undies, but it was better safe than sorry.

Raina opened her closet and pulled out the dress she'd also bought during that very same shopping spree. She'd been waiting for the right occasion to wear it. It was a one-shoulder garnet-colored dress ruched at the waist and ruffled out to stop just above her knee. The garnet color was striking and certainly eye-catching, but it was subdued enough to make it appear she wasn't trying too hard.

She slid the dress over her body and then stared at herself in the mirror. She was wearing her hair down and hopefully she had enough mousse in it to keep the waves in check for the evening. But she was still missing something.

She added some dangling red earrings, a matching necklace and a red clutch purse and she was all set. She bent her head to one side and studied herself. She looked darn good. Spencer would be shocked. He hadn't seen her in anything other than jeans or casual clothes. He was certainly in for a treat. But then again, so was she. She was going out on a date with a sexy, handsome former basketball star. Oh Lord, what had she gotten herself into?

Spencer smiled as he drove to Raina's home. He'd finally convinced the woman to go out on a real date with him. He couldn't remember the last time he'd had to work so hard to convince a woman to spend time with him. Many women just threw themselves at him, so it was refreshing to have to work at it. But Raina was more than a challenge to him. There was something about her feisty spirit that appealed to him and he wanted to know more about her.

Of course, he was immensely attracted to Raina. She tried to hide her curves under unflattering jeans and plaid shirts, but he'd had the opportunity to touch her, to caress her, and knew there was more lying underneath than she portrayed. Her genuine shyness and certain naïveté about life were turn-ons. He was looking forward to corrupting her. He smiled to himself.

But first he would have to romance her, charm her and show her he wasn't the rogue she'd read about online. He was a changed man. And he had the perfect way to do it.

The Alvin Ailey dance troupe was in town and he'd secured two tickets on the main floor. They would enjoy dinner beforehand at a small restaurant he'd discovered in Brickell. The restaurant had great views of the bay and with its muted lighting and candles offered the perfect romantic setting.

Tonight, Raina Martin would not be able to escape him. She was going to let her guard down so he could get close. Because his gut told him Raina was the kind of woman that came along once in a lifetime and he wasn't about to let her go.

"Wow!" Spencer's mouth gaped open when Raina opened the door to let him into her home. "You look amazing." His eyes traveled from her face, which she'd enhanced with makeup, to the swell of her breasts in the garnet dress, then down her hips and her calves and then back up again.

His praise caused a confident smile to spread across Raina's face as she looked at him. "Thank you. Would you like to come in?"

"Sure, but we can't stay long. Our reservation is for six and we have a very tight deadline."

"Are we going someplace after?"

Spencer looked at her. "But of course. You didn't think we were just going to dinner, especially with you in that dress." He motioned to her outfit. "We have to go someplace special." He followed her inside the foyer and looked around.

She watched him eye her living room, which was done in earth colors. A burnt orange sectional sat against one wall with several throw pillows, and a fifty-inch television, various art pieces and tons of photos of her, Alexa and Zoe were set against another. She wanted Zoe to always remember Alexa.

"Very nice," he commented. "So where's Zoe?"

"Summer came to pick her up for a sleepover."

Spencer raised a brow at the sleepover. She saw the wheels turning in his head about the implications of what that meant, but he didn't say anything.

He followed her down the hall and into a state-of-the-art kitchen with maple cabinets, a stainless steel two-door refrigerator with freezer underneath, a gas range with a grill in the center, a double oven and convection in the wall and a huge island in the center with plenty of room for chopping vegetables.

She watched him walk over to the wooden table and

bench that were in her breakfast nook and surrounded by a slew of bay windows. "This is great, Raina." He smoothed his large masculine hands across the grainy surface. "Where did you find it?"

"At this farmhouse Summer and I visited when we were looking for some organic ingredients."

"It's a showstopper," he said. "But then again I expected nothing less of a chef such as you."

Raina chuckled and touched her chest. "Although I was classically trained, I still have a lot to learn."

Spencer turned to her. "Well you obviously are doing something great. Your catering business is the top in the market."

"Word of mouth," she offered.

"There's nothing better," he responded. "You ready to go?"

"Absolutely," Raina said. After she'd grabbed her shawl and clutch purse, they headed out the front door.

Raina was surprised Spencer was driving the Bentley. For some reason, she'd expected he'd be eager to show her his wealth by driving another expensive car.

He opened the car door for her and she slid inside. Her stomach was a ball of nerves as Spencer climbed inside, turned on the ignition and took off.

"Don't be nervous," Spencer said, touching her hand. It was as if he could sense her unease sitting across from him in the passenger side. "I don't bite."

"You sure about that?" she asked, eyeing him from beneath hooded lashes.

He glanced at her quickly and smiled. "Yes. And if you hadn't kept putting me off so long, we would already have had our first date by now and you'd be accustomed to me."

Raina doubted that was even possible. Spencer had an energy that overwhelmed her. Whenever she was around him, he sucked all the air out of the room.

They drove the rest of the way to the restaurant at times in a comfortable silence and others commenting about places they were passing by on the drive. Raina learned that Spencer came from a small area of Miami, Opa-locka. She was eager to learn more about his childhood, but they'd already exited the ramp and several minutes later were pulling up to the valet at the restaurant.

Raina barely got the door open before Spencer strode over to her side to help her out of the car. She looked around. Spencer had chosen well; the restaurant had a picturesque view of the Brickell waterfront.

"C'mon." Spencer tucked her arm in his and they walked up the incline to the hotel where the Latin restaurant with a flair for international cuisine was housed.

Spencer gave his name and soon the hostess was showing them to their seats. "I hope you don't mind that I chose outside seating," he said. "It's such a lovely night, I thought it would be nice."

"Don't mind at all."

After passing by several round tables covered with white tablecloths, the hostess sat them in a secluded alcove on the cobblestone patio overlooking the bay.

Raina sat down, accepted the menu and was perusing it when she noticed Spencer staring at her.

"What?" she asked.

"You." His stare was bold as he assessed her frankly. "I'm not used to seeing you all glammed up. I like it. I like it a lot."

His words were husky with desire, and the smoldering flame in his eyes caused her stomach to flutter. Raina wasn't used to a man showing such blatant sexual desire for her, and it both excited and scared her. "You look very handsome, as well," was all she could manage.

Spencer smiled. "Why, thank you."

The waiter came and Spencer without hesitation ordered them each a Caipirinha. "I promise you'll love it," he said at her raised brow. "It's their specialty drink."

"Can't wait to try it." Raina reached for the glass of water the waiter had filled before his departure to wet her dry throat. She felt like a breathless girl of eighteen. She willed her breathing to calm down to a more even rhythm. After several minutes, she tried to move the conversation to something safer. "In the car, you mentioned you were from Miami. Tell me more."

It seemed as if Spencer gathered she was trying to escape the intensity of his stare, so he humored her. "Yes, Opa-locka is a small community. Cameron and I grew up very poor. And while most of the teenage boys our age were getting into drugs and guns or going into the military, basketball was a way out for me. And Cameron, well he always idolized me and soon we were playing basketball together."

"Your life sounds very different from mine," Raina replied. "I grew up in Miami. My sister and I were very sheltered. We went to a private Catholic school until high school. And I must tell you public school was a rude awakening."

Spencer laughed. "I bet. I, on the other hand, knew nothing else. And when I got a scholarship to go to college, it was a blessing. When Cameron followed in my footsteps a year later, my father couldn't have been prouder."

Raina noticed he hadn't mentioned his mother, but the waiter returned with their drinks.

"Cheers." Spencer held up his drink. "To a wonderful night."

"To a wonderful night." After clicking his glass, Raina took a sip of her Caipirinha and glanced out to the bay. The sun was starting to set and soon they saw the twinkles of lights from the whitewashed Miami buildings. "Hmm, this is so good. What's in it?"

"Cachaça, a special kind of sugarcane rum, lime and sugar," Spencer said, having a taste of the drink, as well.

Raina's eyes grew bright. "I like it."

The waiter came and she ordered a spinach, goat cheese and butternut squash salad while Spencer chose the wedge salad. Entrées of shrimp with wild mushroom risotto and applewood-smoked short ribs with white truffle mashed potatoes soon followed.

Their conversation picked up where it had left off before they were interrupted. Raina learned that Spencer's mother had died of a brain aneurysm when he was six years old. Spencer had never gotten the chance to really know his mother, and Raina felt sad for him. His father had raised him and his brother before his death ten years ago of a heart attack. And she'd thought losing her sister to cervical cancer was a tragedy, but at least she'd had all those years with her.

No wonder he understood loss, because he'd had to endure it at such a young age. And then to lose his brother so suddenly was quite tragic. It made her see yet another side to Spencer. He was no longer the man the media portrayed him to be. There was depth underneath that bulking six-foot-four frame.

Before long, they were finishing their dinner and leaving for the auditorium. Over the meal, Spencer had informed her he had tickets for them to watch Alvin Ailey's dance company. Raina had always wanted to see them and was amused to find out Spencer liked cultural activities just as much as she did.

The dancers were wonderful and their seats were close enough that she could see them quite clearly. Two hours later, she and Spencer were headed back to the car. The night was still young as they walked to the garage. Raina hadn't protested when Spencer had reached for her hand as they'd walked. In fact, she was somewhat restless and didn't understand why.

Spencer must have been, too. No sooner had they exited the elevator, than he spun her into a dark corner of the garage, backed her up against the wall and swooped down to capture her lips in a kiss that awoke all the pent-up sexual frustration she felt for him. The kiss was like the soldering heat that joined metals. His mouth covered hers hungrily, and she grasped at the lapels of his suit jacket as he masterfully caressed her lips with his. She freely gave herself up to the passion, returning his ardor. He understood her cue and his tongue dived inside to duel with hers.

Raina's senses reeled as if short-circuited and she forgot she was making out with Spencer in a very public garage. She just knew that a delightful shiver of wanting was running through her and her instinctive response was to give in to him. It certainly didn't help that he was grinding his hot, pulsing manhood against her and in her flimsy dress she could *feel* him. Her dress crept up her thighs and his hands were everywhere, touching, caressing and molding her soft curves into his hard body.

Spencer's mouth left hers and he showered her lips, then her jaw and then finally her earlobes with kisses. He licked and teased her earlobe and she moaned in response. "Baby, we need to get out of here," he murmured into her ear. "Otherwise, I'm going to have you right here in this garage."

Raina's entire being was trembling and all she could do was nod her consent. Slowly, he pulled away from her, smoothing down her dress, which had risen up around her thighs.

Later, Raina couldn't remember how she made it to the car or the ride to Spencer's penthouse in downtown Miami. All she remembered was the ride in his private elevator, where again they couldn't keep their hands off each other and she succumbed to the tantalizing persuasion of his kiss. By the time they were inside his penthouse; she was burning with desire and had an aching need to be possessed by Spencer.

He swept her in his arms as if she were light as a feather and climbed the stairs to his bedroom. Raina didn't take time to look around the beautifully decorated master bedroom. All she saw was the massive bed in the center of the room; she was sure it had been custom built to accommodate Spencer's size.

He laid her on the bed and she watched him snatch off the tie he wore and fling it and his suit jacket across the room. He flicked his designer loafers off his feet, and Raina rose to her knees and motioned him forward.

He allowed her to unbutton his shirt, one button at a time. It seemed like an eternity before she could finally rid him of it and splay her hands across his hairless chest. His chest was broad, hard and masculine, and she couldn't resist bending her head to flick her tongue across one of his nipples.

"Dear God, Raina." He grasped her by the hair, forcing her to look up at him. "Do you know how much I want you?"

She didn't want to talk. She answered him by brushing her mouth across his while her hands reached for his belt buckle. She made quick work of loosening it so she could unzip his trousers.

"Someone's very eager," Spencer said as he stepped away and out of his pants. He joined Raina on the bed in nothing but his briefs, and she wound her trembling arms around his neck and pulled him down on top of her.

One of his large hands rested on her waist and he drew her to him so she could feel just how hard she'd made him. Raina buried her face in his throat as he kissed her forehead and then her eyebrows and jaw before coming back to her lips.

"I don't want to rush this," Spencer said, caressing her cheek as he looked deeply into her eyes. "If you're not sure…"

She knew why he was asking. She was still fully clothed and if she wanted to pull away, now was the time. It was probably completely out of character for her to act so boldly, but she wanted to be with Spencer and she was willing to take that chance. "I want you, too." Her voice was barely a whisper, but Spencer heard her.

She heard him take a deep breath. "Then let's slow this down," he said. "I don't want our first time together to be rushed. I want it to be memorable."

"Oh, I'm sure it will be." She smiled wickedly, just

as she felt the cool air hit her back. Spencer had unzipped her dress. Raina doubted she would ever forget the dress and what it symbolized.

He eased the satiny fabric down her shoulders to her waist and then skimmed it over her hips and thighs until he was able to toss it to the floor. Raina was left in the lacy undies she'd had the good foresight to wear. Had she subconsciously wanted this to happen?

Her mind reeled because Spencer was fondling each of her breasts, massaging and molding them with his large hands. The gentle massage sent currents of desire flowing through her and when he eased the lace cup of her demi bra aside so his lips could tease and tongue her nipples one breast at a time, Raina began to pant uncontrollably. Each nipple swelled to pebble hardness at his gentle touch. Soon her bra had followed the same path as her panties.

It had been too long since she'd felt this way and it was deliciously sinful. While his tongue did wicked things to her breasts, his hands seared a path across her belly and then down her thighs. One of his hands came to rest on her bikini panties and with both thumbs he tugged and pulled them down her legs.

Then he leaned up to kiss her again. When his tongue slipped inside her mouth past the barrier of her teeth, she reveled in his glorious mouth as he tasted her completely, thoroughly. He lavished her with long, aching strokes that made her weak with need. While his mouth feasted on hers, his hands roamed her body. When he came to the dark curls at the center of her, Raina held her breath in anticipation.

He glanced up at her. "Open your legs," he murmured hotly against her mouth.

Raina did as she was instructed.

Spencer's strong masculine hands were gentle at first as he parted the folds of her womanhood and stroked her clitoris. But then his dexterous fingers began to stroke her faster and faster, in and out, until waves of pleasure raced through her body. Her breath quickened as he moved deeper and deeper inside her. Her fulfillment came quickly, and Raina lost control, crying out and trembling.

"Please," she pleaded shamelessly for him to come inside her, but he wouldn't. His kisses left her mouth once again, this time trailing over her breasts to her stomach to the inside of her thighs. He set her afire everywhere he went. And when his mouth replaced his hands at her core, Raina thrashed against the pillows.

Her heart was pumping so hard and so fast, she was sure he could hear it. He slowly teased her again and again with his tongue, hitting the spot that throbbed for more. Pleading noises escaped her quivering lips as pleasure crashed into her. His mouth began working its way back up her body and a languid feeling coursed through Raina. A feeling she wanted to bestow on Spencer as he'd done to her.

When he tried to gather her in his arms, she pushed him backward against the pillows and sat on her knees. "Whoa, what's going on here?" he asked huskily.

Raina didn't answer; her fingers grasped his hard, hot length and Spencer let out a soft gasp. She lowered her head and slicked her lips over the top of his shaft. She licked him until he buried his hands in her hair and began chanting her name.

"Raina, oh sweet, Raina..."

She pulled him deeper inside her mouth and he

groaned loudly. She continued teasing him with her mouth until he tugged her up by her shoulders and swiftly changed positions so she was lying flat on her back. He was gone for what seemed like seconds before her eyes popped open to see him roll a condom onto his hard length.

"I want you so much," Spencer said, returning to the bed and covering his body with hers. He took one of her hands in his and brought it to his lips.

"Then have me," Raina whispered.

Spencer put her index finger in his mouth just as his knee nudged her legs apart and he settled between her thighs. Raina felt pressure when the tip of his shaft nudged her core. As he moved slowly inside her, stroking her, once, twice and then out, his mouth sucked her finger.

When he lowered her finger from his mouth, Raina lost herself in the intense physical connection she was sharing with him. She'd tried to deny the chemistry she'd felt for Spencer the moment she'd met him, but nothing had prepared her for this kind of mind-blowing sex. His mouth covered hers again as he thrust deeper inside her.

"Feels so good…" Spencer growled through clenched teeth. Beads of sweat were forming on his brow as he stroked her with his tongue and then reached between her legs to methodically stroke her clitoris with his fingers.

It felt so amazing, Raina thought she might die. Instead she shuddered as her climax overtook her and spirals of pleasure surrounded her. Spencer tensed and then he let go and they fell off the end of the world together.

Chapter 7

Raina jolted awake, totally disoriented for several moments until she turned to see Spencer's sleeping form. Oddly enough, she felt satisfied. She'd worn him out with her insatiable appetite. They must have made love three times over the course of the night. She'd never had such an instant and strong attraction to a man before, the way she had with Spencer. And she'd acted on it.

It was completely out of character; she just hoped she didn't live to regret her actions. A lot had transpired in the past few months. She'd lost her sister, met Spencer and she'd slept with him on their first date. Athletes, even former ones, were known to love 'em and leave 'em. Look at her poor sister. Raina hoped it wasn't the case with Spencer and that he hadn't been eager to bed her because she'd been a challenge to him. And now that the challenge was over, she prayed it wouldn't be a "see you later" situation.

Raina rose from the bed and pulled on Spencer's shirt that was lying on the floor. She went into the bathroom to check herself out. Her eyes quickly scanned Spencer's masculine bathroom with its dark marble tile countertops and double sinks. She also noted the cherrywood cabinets and plush black terrycloth towels. In the corner was a sunken tub and separate travertine shower with multiple showerheads. A fluffy white rug sat on the floor. Raina imagined herself making love to Spencer on it and quickly dismissed the thought. She had to take care of her appearance first.

She was horrified by the sight that greeted her in the mirror. Her already wild mane of wavy hair was sticking up in every direction and her perfectly done makeup from the night before was smeared across her face. She looked as if she'd been thoroughly made love to last night.

Raina smiled to herself. She had been. Spencer had been talented and giving. He'd made sure she'd come each time they were together before he did. He'd shown amazing self-restraint. She wanted to do something special for him. After finding a spare toothbrush in the drawer and brushing her teeth, Raina padded down the hardwood stairs to whip up some breakfast for the two of them. She found the kitchen on the bottom level of the penthouse.

It was modern and completely functional with tons of cabinetry. He had a double-sided stainless steel refrigerator and a flat-top stove. Next to it was a built-in microwave and oven surrounded by the beautiful marble countertops that she'd seen in the bathroom upstairs.

She opened the refrigerator and found her options were limited. Clearly Spencer didn't shop too often. But there were some eggs, cheese, asparagus, tomatoes and onions in the fridge. She would make a quick frittata.

Opening the cupboard, she found a bowl, whisk and skillet and some coffee and set about preparing their breakfast. The coffee was brewing and she was pouring the egg mixture into the skillet when she felt a presence behind her.

Spencer was standing in the kitchen watching her and wearing only his boxer briefs. He looked devilishly handsome and Raina's heart skipped a beat.

Spencer's steady gaze traveled over her face and he searched her eyes for some sign of regret about how last night had ended. He found none and his breathing eased.

She happily said, "Good morning," and turned to check on her frittata.

Without speaking, Spencer came from the breakfast bar to circle his arms around her waist and turn her around so he could bring his mouth crushing down on hers. When he finally raised his head, he said, "Good morning." He pulled away to stare at Raina, not letting her go. "Are you okay?"

"Of course." She patted his arm away and turned to lift her frittata slightly out of the skillet with a spatula. Satisfied with how it was cooking, she turned off the burner and placed the skillet in the oven to finish up.

"Are you sure about that?" Spencer inquired, leaning against the counter. "I know our relationship moved rather quickly last night and—"

Before he could finish his sentence, Raina cut him off. "Is that what we have? A relationship?" She went to one of his cabinets and pulled out two plates and two glass tumblers.

Spencer frowned. "Do you think what happened last night was a fluke? And that I only want one night with you?" He went to the coffee machine and poured coffee into a mug that Raina had set nearby. He took a quick sip.

"Honestly, Spencer, I don't know what you want or what I want. A lot has transpired in the past few months. I lost my sister, tried to locate my niece's father only to find out he's deceased and that she now has an uncle with whom I've just had sex with. So forgive me if I'm not ready to analyze this just yet. I just need time to process it all, okay?"

"Of course." Spencer held up his hands and walked over to sit on one of the padded stools at his breakfast nook. "I understand." He didn't want to push her, but he also wanted Raina to know that she wasn't another notch on his bedpost. "When do you think I can see Zoe?"

"Why?" Raina asked. She lifted the frittata from the oven with oven mitts she'd found in a drawer. She cut two pieces and placed them on plates.

"Because I'd like to see her," Spencer replied, taking another sip of his coffee. "And we need to tell her who I am."

Raina spun around to face him. "No, we don't." She set one plate on the counter in front of him and then came and sat down beside him with the other plate.

"Why not?"

Raina swiveled on the stool to look at him. "Spencer, now isn't the right time to spring this on her. She's still dealing with losing Alexa. We don't need to throw more things at her—she's only six years old."

He sighed and glanced at her. "I recognize that, and we should do so delicately with you and I sitting there. Zoe needs to know that she has more family than just the Martins. It might help ease her pain." He knew what it was like to lose a parent at such a young age and knew how it would have helped him if he'd had an aunt, another woman to look to as a mother figure. He could be that father figure to Zoe.

"I think it's too soon." She cut a piece of frittata and took a bite.

"What are you afraid of, Raina?" Spencer inquired. "Of Zoe getting to know me? Or of me being more of a presence in your life? Zoe is my niece, and I would like to get to know her."

"Well, I'm her legal guardian and I'm telling you now is the wrong time."

"Why must you be so contrary, Raina?" He angrily stabbed at the frittata she'd made with his fork before pushing some in his mouth and chewing. When she didn't answer, he finally added, "I'm not asking your permission on whether or not I can see my own niece."

Raina's eyes sharpened and she stood up from the breakfast bar. "Well if that's the way you want to play this." She stormed out of the kitchen.

Spencer stared at her retreating form as she climbed the stairs to the master bedroom. The conversation had not gone as he'd intended. He'd wanted to wake up with her and make love again to her pliant body until she was moaning out his name as she'd done last night. Now any chance of that was ruined because he'd tried to strong-arm her like he did with his sports owners. And he'd failed miserably.

Spencer left the table and took the stairs two at a time to reach Raina. He didn't want their time together to end this way, not after all they'd shared last night. He heard running water and found Raina in the shower. She was dipping her head under the showerhead and he watched as the glistening beads of water drifted down her curvaceous body. His shaft instantly began to harden. On impulse, Spencer threw open the shower door.

Startled Raina turned around, covering her bosom with her hands. Before she could utter a single word of protest, he climbed inside and his hands splayed over her back and pressed her body firmly to him. His mouth claimed hers with the arrogance of a pirate claiming an innocent virgin. His hard readiness ploughed against her middle, and he began rubbing against her with erotic undulations. He wanted her to feel how hard she'd made him even when he was upset and wanted to throttle her.

"Spencer." Raina sighed when he planted his hot mouth at the base of her throat and kissed his way down her chest. When he came to her breasts, his tongue became a wet tormenter as he worked his way from one breast to the other. He bathed her areolae until they peaked and began to pout and thrust into his eager lips.

He lifted Raina's hips over him. He wanted to take her right there in the shower, but he knew he had to protect them, and he had a box of condoms in a drawer underneath one of the sinks. He turned off the taps and murmured, "I want you now, please." She answered by wrapping her legs around his hips.

Spencer grasped her slick buttocks in his hands and pushed the shower door open with one foot. With Raina still in his arms, he walked over to the drawer and with one hand fumbled to find the box of condoms. When he did, he grabbed a foil packet and lowered their wet bodies onto the white rug at the foot of the tub.

He stared down at Raina. Her jet-black wavy hair spread out on the white rug was oddly erotic and he couldn't wait to take her. He wasted no time tearing open the foil packet and sheathing himself.

He leaned forward so he could pay tribute to her body by kissing and licking her arms, her breasts, her elbows, her belly and the top of her thighs. Spencer hit every erogenous zone of Raina's body until he came to the center of her heat. He hovered over her, teasing her. "Do you want me, Raina?"

"Yes, yes," she moaned.

With his mouth he took liberties with her sex, tonguing her until he stoked the fires of her body. She began to tremble beneath him and that's when he knew she was ready. He braced himself above her and Raina parted her legs, eager to receive him. His body sank into hers and she curled her legs around his hips, allowing her sweet haven to entrap him in pure bliss. He began to thrust deeper and deeper inside her. She matched his movements by bucking underneath him and he stroked her from the inside until he began to sway... to peak and he was finally swept away.

"Raina, did you hear what I said?" Summer asked.

"What was that?" Raina asked, blinking several times. She'd been unable to focus since she'd arrived at Summer's place to pick up Zoe. Her mind kept wandering back to making love to Spencer on the white rug in his bathroom. *What the heck is wrong with me?* Had she been that hard up for sex that she would let him take her right there on the floor?

But she had. And it had been the most erotic, the most sensual sex she'd ever had. The feel of the soft fibers of the rug against her backside, the feel of his warm hands on her body, the feel of Spencer's tongue as he licked her, the feel of his hard shaft buried deep inside her had been incredibly hot. How could she have let him make love to her when she'd been angry with him?

"I said that Zoe was a trouper last night," Summer repeated herself, but she wasn't sure her best friend was listening because she had a faraway look in her eyes, which left Summer to wonder if something more had happened with Spencer other than dinner last night.

"Oh, I'm so glad she was no trouble," Raina said, grabbing Zoe's overnight bag and slinging it over her shoulder. "I appreciate you taking her last night. My parents had a prior engagement they couldn't get out of." She turned to her niece, who was still sitting on the sofa playing a video game with Ryan.

"It was no trouble at all," Summer said, grabbing Raina's sleeve and pulling her into the foyer of her apartment. "So you want to tell me what happened last night?"

"What do you mean?" Raina asked absentmindedly.

"Never mind. We'll talk tomorrow when your head isn't in the clouds."

"Oh, great, thanks," Raina said. "Zoe, let's go. I have a lot of errands today."

A few minutes later, they were in her car. Raina's cell phone rang. The display read Spencer's number and Raina's heart began to pound frantically.

Spencer Davis was making her do all kind of firsts

and behaving erratically. She needed some time to process everything that was going on between them. Not to mention she was sure Spencer was not about to back off from seeing Zoe or telling her his true identity. So she let his call go to voice mail. She would talk to him in due time. For now, she needed to put everything that had occurred between them in perspective as well as set up a meeting with her lawyer. She needed to know exactly where she stood.

Spencer clicked the end button on his cell phone. He'd gotten Raina's voice mail. She was avoiding him, and he didn't like it. He needed to talk to her, hear her voice and let her know that there was more than enough room in Zoe's life for the both of them. There didn't have to be one person or the other, but she was stubborn.

He'd thought after they'd made love on the bathroom floor that her attitude may have changed, but he'd soon realized his mistake. Afterward, they'd stayed joined for several long minutes before she'd disengaged herself and headed back into the shower. She'd told him she'd like to take a shower alone and he hadn't argued. When she'd reemerged; she'd told him that it was clear he had a way with women, with her, but that he would not be able to seduce her into compliance. Then she'd quickly left his penthouse.

Spencer felt they were in no better place than they'd been in earlier and perhaps worse because she probably felt like she was powerless when she was around him, which he didn't want. He wanted her to *want* to be with him. Raina was the first woman who'd ever made him think about the future and what it would be like to have her in his life. But how could he convince her that they had something special? He would have to figure out a way to get through to Raina and break down the defenses she had around her heart.

He was at a loss and needed someone to talk to, so he dialed Ty's number. Ty answered after several moments. "Hey, what's up?"

"You busy?" Spencer inquired.

"No, Brielle and I just came in from running and I was about to hop in the shower. What's going on?"

"Raina Martin."

"Ah." Ty sighed on the other end as if he knew what Spencer was about to say. "The chef you met that night at the charity event. So she's got you all twisted, huh?"

"Man, you don't know the half of it."

"Talk to me."

"Well, you remember she turned me down, right?"

"Yeah, what about it?"

"A few days later, I got served with paternity papers by who else?"

"Raina?" Ty asked disbelievingly.

"One and the same."

"Dude, did you forget you'd tapped that?"

"Of course not," Spencer replied huffily. "She was trying to find out if I'd fathered her *sister's* child."

"And did you?"

"Hell no!" Spencer yelled. "But—" he paused for several beats "—Cameron did."

"Get out of here!"

"No joke." Spencer couldn't believe the turn of events, either. It was as if fate had played some cosmic joke on him.

"Your brother? Are you sure? Did you have a paternity test taken?" Ty started firing questions at him.

Spencer nodded on the other end as if Ty could see him. "Yup, I humored her and took one myself since Raina believed me to be the father, but then I secretly had one done with Cam's DNA and it was a match."

"Oh, Lord. Wait a second, why was Raina asking you to take the paternity test? Where is her sister?"

"She died a few months ago of cancer."

"Wow! That's rough. Poor thing is an orphan. So what now?"

"I don't know, man. That's why I'm calling you," he responded. "In the short time I've known Raina we've become rather...er, close...if you know what I mean."

"I do." Ty didn't need it spelled out for him. His boy Spencer was a ladies' man, though he had been re-formed the past few years. "Add the fact you and she now share a niece and that sounds rather complicated."

"Ya think?" Spencer snorted. "And Raina wants to put her head in the sand and not deal with the facts. She's Zoe's guardian now and is making all the deci-sions, but Zoe is my niece, too. And I want to get to know her. She's Cameron's child, for Christ's sake, and *my only living relative.*"

"Listen," Ty said reasonably. "Didn't you just say a lot has happened in a couple of weeks? Perhaps she just needs time for her brain to catch up with her emotions. She didn't strike me as a woman who acts on impulse."

"And what am I supposed to do in the meantime?" Spencer inquired. "I've already wasted precious time with Zoe. She's already lost her mother, and when she learns she doesn't have a father, either, she'll need me."

"Then be there, but don't just insert yourself into their lives." But Ty was talking to deaf ears. Spencer only knew how to attack life at full force. It was how he'd always been on the court when he's played basketball. He would attack the boards hard and get those extra points that the team desperately needed.

"You make that sound easy," Spencer said.

"It can be," Ty said. "You weren't even thinking about dating, much less a relationship, and now that you've met Raina, all of a sudden you're ready to attack her with everything you've got. Slow down and let her catch up to you."

"I hear you," Spencer said. "And I'll try." He ended the call. He'd reached out to Ty for some sound advice, but he wasn't sure he could follow all of it. If he backed off now, it might make Raina think Zoe wasn't important to him. Worse yet, she might think he'd used her for kicks and was done with her. No, he had to continue on the same course, just with a little more diplomacy.

Chapter 8

"Do you really think Spencer has a chance to win custody of Zoe?" Raina asked her attorney the following day, her anxiety rising. She'd made the mistake of allowing her parents to attend the session with her and matters had gone from bad to worse.

"You're on solid standing, Raina," her attorney replied. "You've had a relationship with Zoe since she was a baby and you were legally named Zoe's guardian by the court after Alexa's death."

"But," her mother interjected, "what aren't you saying?"

Raina wished she'd come by herself to the meeting, but after she'd told her parents the situation and that Spencer was Zoe's uncle and not her father, they'd been determined to accompany her. Her mother had been so scared of Spencer taking Zoe away that she'd become hysterical. Raina had figured the only way to calm her down was to have her hear it from the horse's mouth that Raina had a good case if it should go to court.

"I'm going to be honest with you, Mrs. Martin. Mr. Davis does have some rights here. He could claim that Alexa purposely kept the fact that Zoe was his daughter from his brother."

"But that's not true." Crystal cried into her tissue. "My baby would never have done that. If Cameron Davis didn't know he had a daughter, it was because he didn't deserve to know or didn't want to know."

"We don't know that for sure, Mama," Raina said. "We don't know what happened between Alexa and Cameron."

"Why are you defending him?" her mother responded harshly.

"I'm not," Raina replied, wringing her hands. "I'm just saying that at the time, Alexa wasn't always forthcoming. You remember how wild she was. She was a party girl."

"Exactly," her attorney said, pointing to Raina. "If Mr. Davis does some digging, he could pounce on that." At Crystal's sobs, he tried to sound more reassuring. "Listen, Mrs. Martin, it is highly unlikely Mr. Davis would ever win custody of your granddaughter."

"But he could take Raina to court," her father finally spoke up. He'd been listening quietly and absorbing all the facts.

"Yes. Most likely he would end up with visitation rights."

"Visitation!" Her mother jumped up. "He doesn't deserve visitation. His brother wasn't even a part of Zoe's life. They've done nothing for her like we have."

She motioned to her husband, leaving Raina out. "They haven't consoled Zoe on losing her mother. We're Zoe's family."

"I'm sorry," the attorney replied.

"I guess visitation isn't so bad." Raina tried to look at the positive. She would still retain primary custody and keep her promise to Alexa to take care of her child.

"Are you so ready to turn Zoe over to that man that you've lost your mind?" her mother wailed.

"Crystal!" Her father sat up and her mother looked down as if she'd been scolded.

Her mother's words stung and Raina tried not to feel hurt, but it was hard not to and a hot tear rolled down her cheek. "You have not been raising Zoe by yourself, Mother. *I* have been taking care of her since Alexa's death. Hell, for longer. Since she was hospitalized, so don't you dare act like I'm ready to abandon Zoe. And as for Spencer, he's done nothing but be cooperative, even when we accused him of being Zoe's father. He took the paternity test voluntarily."

Her mother was only mildly embarrassed by her outburst and commented, "But didn't you say he secretly ran an unauthorized test with his brother's DNA. Can't we require a new one?"

"Absolutely," the attorney replied. "We can demand one. But if it yields the same results, I would suggest you consider settling on a visitation schedule with Mr. Davis." He looked directly at Raina when he spoke. "Why incur unnecessary legal fees?"

"No!" Her mother rose.

"Mother, please," Raina implored. She hadn't quite decided what she wanted to do, but she certainly wasn't going to be walked over by her parents or Spencer.

"Mrs. Martin, this is Raina's decision." The attorney spoke quietly. "Ultimately, she's Zoe's legal guardian."

"I know you're upset with me," her mother cried and bent down on her knees. "And I know I spoke harshly. You know I didn't mean it." She looked up into her eyes. "Please don't do this, Raina. Fight. Fight for Zoe. You owe Alexa this."

Raina stared at her niece through the windows as Zoe danced her way across the hardwood floors in her weekly jazz dance class. Zoe was quite the little performer and loved to be seen. She was glad Zoe had an outlet considering everything she'd been through. Other than a few crying spells, Zoe was holding up surprisingly well. *What was the saying, kids are resilient?* Raina was finding that to be true.

Raina wished she could say the same. Ever since her night with Spencer, she'd felt anything but resilient. Instead, she felt like she was a pile of mush. The man was captivating her dreams at night and invading her days with visions of their lovemaking. So much so that she was having a hard time focusing. Summer had commented as much earlier that day as they'd prepped for an upcoming catering event.

Summer had finally gotten Raina to spill the beans and reveal that she and Spencer had spent the night together. Summer hadn't been surprised by her spontaneity, and she was excited that Raina was finally living a little. Raina, on the other hand, wished she'd shown more reserve. Spencer probably thought he had her wrapped around his finger. She hadn't just slept with him on the first date, but multiple times and on his bathroom floor! Raina colored as if any of the other mothers who were watching their children could read her thoughts. It was happening again; her mind was wandering to him.

Raina thought about what her attorney had said. She was on sound footing because Alexa was Zoe's legal parent and Cameron Davis wasn't even listed on the birth certificate. Add to that Alexa had a will that stated she wanted Raina to raise Zoe and Raina had been given legal guardianship by the court, which made for a very good defense. But the paternity test Spencer had done would easily show Cameron was the father. And although Spencer may not have known Zoe or had a relationship with her, he could make a very good case for visitation rights or even shared custody.

Could Raina let that happen? Alexa had left Zoe in her care, and she didn't want to let her down. Raina felt guilty for opening up this can of worms. She'd just been trying to give her niece the one thing she craved: a father.

"Zoe is great, isn't she?"

Raina's stomach flip-flopped at the sound of Spencer's voice behind her. It was as if he'd materialized right out of her daydreams. *What the heck is he doing here?* Perhaps she was imagining it. She closed her eyes to banish the voice from her head, but he spoke again.

"She's the best dancer in the room," he commented.

It wasn't a dream. Spencer was there at Zoe's dance practice. How had he found them? *Summer.* Slowly, Raina turned around to face the object of her daydreams. "Spencer."

He looked fantastic in a purple pullover sweater and vintage jeans. He was freshly shaved and she could smell a hint of aftershave.

She tried not to notice him too much and nodded curtly before turning back around to watch Zoe.

Spencer joined her at the window and his shoulder bumped hers. "I hope you're not mad."

Is he serious?

"Summer told me where you guys were going to be," Spencer said. "And I had some free time, so I thought I would come see you *both*."

"Well, she had no right to do that," Raina said, giving him a sideways glance. She didn't want to get into a discussion with him in front of all the other mothers. They would all gossip behind her back, and they'd already said enough since Alexa was gone.

"Don't be mad at her. I'm sure she was only trying to help. And I am Zoe's uncle, after all."

"So, you keep reminding me," Raina whispered. She noticed several mothers watching them; a few eyes showed recognition of who he was and openly gawked.

"Listen, Raina, I'm not trying to ram this down your throat." Spencer lowered his voice and spoke in her ear. "I'm just trying to figure out my place in Zoe's life. So, in that spirit, I got us all tickets to go to the Miami Falcons game this Friday night."

Raina turned and glared at him. He was making himself at home in her life as if he had a right to be there. She was used to doing things on her own and didn't like the interference. She took a deep breath and tried to check herself before speaking. "Spencer, that's a lovely gesture, but Zoe and I have—"

"Spence!" Zoe screamed out his name from the doorway of the classroom. Spencer bent to his knees, and Zoe rushed into his arms.

Spencer smiled affectionately as he hugged Zoe

tightly to his chest. He looked up at Raina with tears in his eyes. In that moment, she could see he was hugging her not as a friend like he'd done before, but rather he was seeing her for the first time as his niece, his flesh and blood.

A lump formed in Raina's throat. Spencer had lost his parents and brother. Zoe had to be a reminder that he hadn't completely lost Cameron. Raina's heart softened.

"Where have you been?" Zoe asked. "I've missed you."

Raina was surprised to hear Zoe say that because she'd never said anything to Raina.

"I missed you, too." Spencer rose to his feet and lifted Zoe into his arms.

Zoe laughed as if she didn't believe him. "Did you really?"

"Of course I did, munchkin." Spencer tweaked her nose between his index and middle finger.

"Stop that." Zoe swatted his hand away.

"All right, Zoe." Raina gave her niece a reproachful look and Zoe attempted to look chastised, but when Spencer put his finger in Zoe's ear, she slapped his hand away again playfully. "Am I going to have to separate you two?"

Spencer smiled broadly, showing off his brilliant white teeth. "No, we're just having a little fun. But we could have a lot more." He looked at Raina when he said it and she knew he was talking about the basketball game. Raina was hesitant to be close to Spencer again.

Look at what she'd done the first chance she'd been alone with him. Of course, if she agreed, Zoe would be with them at the basketball game and she would inadvertently serve as a chaperone.

"Who's in the mood for ice cream?" Spencer asked, heading toward the door of the dance school.

Raina could merely wave at the other mothers before rushing out the door behind him. "Zoe can't have ice cream before dinner."

"Why not?"

Raina sighed. Clearly, he'd never been around a rambunctious child who'd had too much sugar before bed. "Because she'll never eat her dinner."

"But she was so good in there," Spencer said, pointing back at the school.

"Did you really think so, Spence?" Zoe asked enthusiastically. "I was trying my best, just like Mommy... Mommy told me to."

When she said the word *mommy* Zoe's eyes began to tear up. Raina was used to these out-of-the-blue moments, had been there for most of them, but Spencer was clearly affected because he held Zoe tighter in his arms.

"It's okay, Zoe." He rubbed her back slowly as sobs began to rack her tiny little body. He looked to Raina, and his eyes asked what he should do, but he was doing it. The counselor had told Raina to expect the grief to catch Zoe unaware and to be ready with love and understanding.

After several excruciating moments, Zoe began to quiet. "How about that ice cream?" Spencer looked at Raina and pleaded with her to agree.

She gave him a halfhearted smile and nodded. "We'll follow behind you," Raina said, pulling Zoe out of his arms and into the comfort of her arms. Seconds later, she was walking to her car and putting Zoe into the backseat. "You okay, pumpkin?" Raina asked.

Zoe merely nodded absently and looked as though she was a million miles away.

As she slid into the driver's seat, Raina noticed Spencer hadn't moved from the spot she'd left him in and was still staring after them.

Spencer drove to an ice-cream shop nearby that had several varieties and toppings. He wanted to do anything he could to cheer up his niece. When she'd begun crying, he'd felt such a tug of protectiveness that it had surprised him. Although Zoe was family, he was just getting to know her, but seeing her in distress had tugged at his heartstrings. He and Raina were older and could deal with losing their siblings, or at least they coped. But Zoe? She was a six-year-old little girl. How did you explain or even get her to comprehend that her mother was never coming back? He applauded Raina and her family for all they'd done for Zoe. Despite everything, she was mostly a happy little girl, and of course that was due in part to Alexa.

Oh, Alexa. Spencer wished he'd given Alexa his brother's new number and that she would have had the courage to tell him he was a father. It may have changed Cameron's outlook on life. But she hadn't and Spencer would have to live with that. He would have to make up for his brother's shortcomings by being the best uncle in the world.

He stopped and parked in a spot outside the front door of the ice-cream shop. Raina's car slid into the space beside him and he rushed over to open the driver's door.

His groin tightened when she exited the vehicle. She was wearing a print cardigan over a simple white top and slim-cut olive corduroy pants with tall boots, and her hair was in her usual ponytail, but she looked sexy as hell to Spencer.

"Thank you." Raina glanced at him and then quickly diverted her eyes as if staring at him would turn her to stone. She opened the back door, and Zoe climbed out.

"So what are you in the mood for?" Spencer said with somewhat forced enthusiasm, eager to get Zoe back in a good mood. "Rocky road? Mint chocolate chip?"

Zoe smiled halfheartedly and he knew she was coming around.

Ten minutes later, they were all sitting down in a booth enjoying their ice cream. He and Zoe were sharing a banana split with all the fixings, while Raina had settled on a raspberry yogurt. Spencer called her a spoilsport, but Raina had merely stuck her tongue out at him and pointed to her hips.

Hips. Curvy hips that Spencer remembered running his hands up and down. Hips that he'd gripped as he'd thrust inside her over and over again. *God, what is wrong with me?* He should be focusing on Zoe and not letting his hormones take over. He blinked several times and returned his attention back to Zoe. They were discussing what Zoe was going dress as for Halloween.

"I think you should be a princess," Raina said.

"Noooo, I've been a princess before," Zoe said huffily. "I want to be a witch."

"A witch?" Spencer asked.

Zoe smiled and her eyes grew big. "Yeah." She nodded enthusiastically. "With a witch hat and a broom."

Spencer burst out laughing and Zoe glared at him as if he'd offended her. If anyone had ever told him that one day he'd be sitting with his niece and the sexiest caterer he'd ever met discussing children's Halloween costumes, he would have told them they were crazy.

"I'm sorry, I'm sorry." Spencer held up his hands in defense. "I think it's a great idea, Zoe. We should go shopping for it."

"That's not really necessary, Spencer," Raina replied. "My mom and I have it covered. We've already made plans for this weekend."

"Oh, of course." Spencer didn't realize he was interloping. He was just trying to be helpful. It was why he'd come to the dance school. He was trying to figure out what was important to Zoe and how he'd fit in. He'd known Raina would not be happy about his presence. And she hadn't been, but she'd seemed to soften when Zoe appeared. "What about what we talked about earlier?" He was trying not to mention the tickets outright so as not to get Zoe's hopes up if Raina axed the idea.

"Zoe, can you go ask the lady at the counter for a cup of water for me?" Raina inquired.

"Okay." Zoe scurried out of the booth and in the direction of the front counter.

Raina eyed Zoe and then quickly turned to Spencer. "You just don't know how to let up, do you?"

"What do you mean?"

"I told you to give me space," Raina said and then turned to glance at Zoe again. "But you just can't do that. You have to come on strong all the time."

"Honestly, it's who I am. I don't know any other way to be."

"That's no excuse," Raina said tersely.

"C'mon, Raina. You don't have to be tough all the

time." Spencer's eyes bore into hers. "It's just a basketball game."

"Fine." Raina shrugged as Zoe returned with her cup of water. "We'll go with you."

"Go with Spence where?" Zoe asked with keen ears.

"Didn't I tell you about listening to grown folk's conversation?" Raina asked, glaring at her niece.

Zoe lowered her head and slid back into the booth. "Yes, ma'am."

Spencer stared at Raina until she finally said, "Spence has invited us to a basketball game. Doesn't that sound like fun?"

"Really, Spence?" Zoe perked back up in her seat.

"Yes, munchkin. I'll be by to pick up you and your aunt Raina on Friday night." He stared at Raina, daring her to say no. He saw her mouth twitch as if to correct him about picking them up, but she must have thought better of it because for once she let it go.

Chapter 9

On Friday night, Spencer was raring to go. He'd made sure to dress casually in jeans and his favorite jersey. He showed up at Raina's door with a matching kid's jersey he'd had made specifically for Zoe. Raina didn't strike him as very much into sports, but he'd had one made for her, too, just in case.

When Raina opened the door, she was a vision. Her long hair hung in wavy curls well past her shoulders. He loved when she wore it down, and he could remember what it was like running his hands through the luxurious mane. She was dressed simply in a gray turtleneck and slim-fitting jeans. She wore hardly any makeup other than a pale shade of lipstick on her delectable lips. Raina had a natural beauty that didn't need embellishments. She could have been wearing a potato sack and he would still find her attractive.

"C'mon in." She motioned him inside. "It's chilly out."

"It sure is," Spencer said, dropping the bag he'd brought onto the floor and rubbing his hands together to warm them up for a minute. Fall was certainly kicking in big-time and the air had turned unseasonably cold almost overnight.

"Zoe's in the living room." Raina turned to go away, but Spencer caught her unaware and pulled her into his arms.

He brushed a soft kiss over her mouth and it elicited more than he'd bargained for because passion ignited. Raina relaxed in his arms and he grabbed her face with both hands and deepened the kiss. His tongue entered her mouth with sweeping thrusts and Raina responded in turn.

Slowly, Spencer tilted his head away to gaze at her. He hadn't meant the kiss to be anything other than a sweet gesture, but whenever he was around Raina she sparked a lust in him that made him feel like a randy teenage boy.

They stared at each other for several long moments, neither of them speaking. It wasn't until they heard Zoe coming down the stairs calling his name that they reluctantly pulled away.

"Spence." Zoe gave his legs a gentle tug when she reached the bottom level. "Where have you been?"

"I'm sorry, munchkin," he said, lifting her into his arms. "Traffic was a nightmare, but there's still plenty of time for us to grab a bite to eat at the restaurant first."

"Let's go," Zoe urged excitedly.

Spencer looked at Raina. "I'm ready," she said, walking over to the coatrack. She pulled off Zoe's lightweight jacket and handed it to him and then slid a suede jacket over her shoulders.

"Wait, wait," Spencer said and sat Zoe on the floor. He reached for the bag he'd discarded earlier in his haste to kiss Raina and reached inside to hand Zoe the jersey.

"Oh," Zoe exclaimed, holding it up to admire. "Can I put it on, Auntie Raina?"

Raina smiled. "Of course." She helped Zoe take off the V-neck sweater she was wearing over her turtleneck, so Zoe could put the jersey on over it. It fit her perfectly. Raina looked at Spencer. "Did you have this custom-made?"

Spencer didn't reply; he only gave her a large grin. "Now you're ready. Let's go."

Thirty minutes later they were parking in the VIP section of the garage near the arena. Once they exited the garage, Spencer and Raina both reached for Zoe's hand as they walked across the street. Spencer saw the surprise in Raina's eyes that he'd had the forethought to think of someone other than himself, but she didn't say anything.

When they arrived at the VIP entrance, Spencer handed the guard the three tickets for floor seats at the arena. "Hey, Spencer. How you doing, man?" The guard gave him a one-armed hug.

"I'm doing good." Spencer patted the man on the back. "Good to see you, Bart."

"How do you know him?" Zoe asked as they walked away.

Spencer again looked at Raina. He wasn't sure how much she wanted him to share about himself. When she inclined her head, he answered. "I used to play for this team."

"You were a basketball player?" Zoe asked.

"He was one of the best." An usher who was putting bands around their wrists spoke up.

Zoe's eyes grew large with excitement. "Were you really?"

Spencer nodded. "Yeah, I was pretty good." He tried to downplay his success as he led Zoe and Raina into the restaurant that was reserved for VIPs and season floor-seat ticketholders.

Zoe's eyes lit up. "Cool!"

Spencer was happy he'd impressed his niece, but he was more concerned about impressing her aunt. Although she'd kissed him back earlier with the same passion, he felt she was still acting aloof toward him. He didn't know how to break through her reserve, but he had to keep trying.

Raina sipped on her house wine as she watched Spencer take Zoe around to the different stations, which had offerings of jerk chicken, jambalaya, sliced roast beef, garlic mashed potatoes and vegetable medleys and hot dogs. There was a make-your-own-taco station filled with all the toppings and condiments. She saw them settle on tacos and was amazed at Spencer's patience as he helped Zoe make her own creation. They both came back with heaping plates including nachos with cheese.

"Are you sure you're going to eat all that, Zoe?" Raina inquired.

"I'm going to try," Zoe said, picking up one of her overstuffed hard shell tacos.

Spencer did the same, and Raina laughed when both their tacos began to fall apart as they ate. "Oh, that's the best part." Spencer picked up the spillage with his fingers. Zoe followed suit, and soon they were laughing up a storm.

Raina was scared at how easily Spencer was fitting into their lives. She'd had so many changes the past few months. How had her normally dull life spun so far out of control?

She knew the answer. It was the moment she'd led with her heart instead of her head and went in search of Zoe's father. Her mother had warned her about opening up Pandora's box, but she'd been so sure that finding Zoe's father was what was best. How could she have known what was in store? Spencer Davis was not going away. He was making his presence known in Zoe's life. Spencer was all her niece could talk about for the past week. Him and how excited she was about the basketball game tonight.

And as for Raina, he'd made his presence in her life known in more ways than one. From the moment they'd met, he'd been relentless in his pursuit of her and now that they shared a common thread, Raina was afraid to see how much further he would go. She was used to being in the shadows. It had been that way her entire life. First with her parents idolizing Alexa as their favorite child, and now in her career as a caterer, she was in the back of the house creating works of art.

She wasn't used to being the center of attention and it made her uncomfortable. She'd never met a man like Spencer. He challenged her at every turn, and it disconcerted her. She wanted to run away. That's what she'd been trying to do, but he refused to let her. He just kept getting in her face like he'd done tonight when he'd kissed her. She hadn't expected it and she'd been off balance ever since.

As if he could sense that she was thinking about him, Spencer looked up. "Did you enjoy dinner?" he asked, looking at her plate of half-eaten jerk chicken and jambalaya.

"Oh, yes." Raina picked up her fork and stabbed at her green beans. She was embarrassed at having been caught daydreaming. "It's delicious." She put a bite in her mouth.

He seemed satisfied with her answer and he and Zoe kept talking and laughing as he regaled her with stories of being in the NBA.

It wasn't long before they were leaving the restaurant and sliding into their floor seats. Raina was first, followed by Zoe, then Spencer.

"It's so big," Zoe said, her eyes scanning the entire expanse of the arena, trying to take in all the sights.

Raina was impressed, too. She'd never been to a live basketball game and she was amazed at how big the arena was and how close they were to the players. Their floor seats were directly behind the Miami Falcons team.

Spencer stepped away for several minutes to talk to some of his old teammates as well as some of his current clients. It gave Raina a few minutes alone with Zoe.

"Are you having fun, sweetheart?" Raina asked, giving Zoe's shoulders a gentle squeeze.

"Oh, Auntie, Spence is the best, isn't he?" Zoe asked, looking up at her.

"You really like him a lot, don't you?"

Zoe nodded. "I do. I think he's the best. He's so fun. It's kind of like having a dad." She said it with such ease and then turned away from Raina to focus back on the court.

All the color drained from Raina's face when she looked up and saw Spencer had rejoined them. It was clear he'd overheard what Zoe said. He probably felt validated by Zoe's admission, but Raina was afraid of losing Zoe. She'd promised Alexa that she'd take care of her.

In that moment, Raina didn't look at Spencer even though she felt his eyes imploring her to look at him. She had to sort this out. But how? What place should Spencer have in her niece's life? And, for that matter, in hers? Shouldn't she be focused on Zoe and getting her through this hard time? Wasn't that what real mothers did? Was she even entitled to think about her own happiness?

A cheer came from the crowd as the game had just begun and Miami had scored the first points. Raina rose from her chair and cheered like Zoe and Spencer, but in her heart she was far from happy. She was torn.

"So, did you take my advice?" Ty asked Spencer when they met up at their favorite sports club to shoot some hoops the following day. It was their way to blow off some steam when Ty was in town.

"Advice?" Spencer acted dumb as he closed the locker and pulled one knee to the bench and laced up his sneakers. He knew what Ty was asking and he'd done the exact opposite of his advice. Not only had he coerced Raina into attending the basketball game, but he'd had Mona arrange to hire Raina's catering company to help throw a party for his clients at his mansion on Star Island.

"Oh, so now you're going to act like you're hard of hearing?" Ty asked, as he stretched his legs on the floor in preparation for their game. They had a tendency to turn heated given both of their competitive streaks.

Spencer sighed. "Sort of."

"What do you mean, 'sort of'?" Ty stopped stretching and glared at him. "Did you go to the boards on the woman like you would a basketball game?"

A frown formed on Spencer's mouth. "Not that hard."

"So you didn't back off and give her the space she needed to come to you?"

"Listen, Ty, I couldn't," Spencer responded, ready to defend his actions. "I've lost too much time with my niece as it is. I have a lot to make up for. So although I didn't come on *too* strong with Raina, I did make her see that my presence in Zoe's life is needed and wanted."

"How's that?"

"Well, when I invited them both to a Miami Falcons game, I overheard Zoe tell Raina that she liked having me around and that I was kind of like a dad."

Ty rose to face Spencer and searched his eyes for the truth. "A dad? Did she use those exact words?"

"She did."

Ty swallowed hard. "Are you sure you're ready for that, man? I mean, I know you like this woman and you want to get to know your niece, but you're getting attached pretty quickly to this ready-made family."

"Is there something wrong with that?"

"No." Ty paused, searching for the right words. "I just think you should be taking things much slower. I mean, you just found out about all of this a few weeks ago and you're ready to change your whole life."

"I know that," Spencer said. "But Zoe needs a male

influence in her life. Are you telling me to keep my distance from her, too?"

"No, of course not," Ty replied. "I'm not telling you not to get to know your niece, but you can be that uncle that comes and gets her once a month for a few hours."

"That's not the kind of uncle I want to be. I want to be more hands-on."

"Spencer, have I ever steered you wrong?" At Spencer's smirk, Ty laughed. "Okay, maybe a few times back when we were kids, but this is different. What happens when you've had your fill of Raina Martin? What then? Imagine how your niece will feel when you start to make yourself scarce."

Spencer couldn't see himself ever tiring of Raina's beauty or spunk, but he let Ty continue.

"Since you want to do something big, something to show you care, set up a trust in Zoe's name. I bet that would make you feel good. And in the meantime, give your head time to catch up with your heart."

Spencer nodded. Ty's idea about a trust was great, and he'd been mulling it over himself. But he doubted he would be able to keep his distance from the Martin women. Not only did Zoe deserve more, but he hadn't gotten his fill of her beautiful aunt. "I hear you, man." Spencer shook Ty's hand. "Now let's go play some ball."

"So, what's our next event?" Raina asked Summer after they'd decided to go out for lunch to discuss the upcoming months' catering gigs. The past few weeks, she'd been much too preoccupied with her situation with Spencer and Zoe to focus much on the business, and Summer had been taking up the slack.

After they'd sat down at the outside café that overlooked the beach, Summer pulled out her iPad to go over Diamonds and Gems Caterings upcoming events. "With the holiday season, reservations have been brisk," she stated. "I think we might have to hire some additional help. Now that you have Zoe, you can't put in the long nights you once did."

"I'm sorry, Summer," Raina apologized.

"It's not an indictment, Raina," Summer replied. "None of us could have predicted Alexa would get sick and you would have to care for your niece. I would never fault you for that. All I'm saying is we've got a few parties coming up and we're going to need a few extra hands on deck."

A waitress came over to their table. "Can I get you ladies something to drink?"

"Diet soda for me," Raina said.

"Water with lemon." Summer swished her finger across her tablet to bring up her calendar.

"I'll be right back with those drinks," the waitress said before she left.

Summer rattled on about all the events she'd scheduled in Raina's absence. "So, we have the Henderson's Halloween party the day before Halloween, Allyson Peters's veteran's party in two weeks and then the Davis Sports Agency party this weekend." She bowed her head and waited for the fallout that was about to come.

Davis Sports Agency? Raina said the words over in her head. Where had she heard the name before? "Davis Sports Agency. Wait a second…" That was Spencer's company. She focused her stare on her partner and waited for a response.

Summer was slow to look up, but eventually her

dark brown eyes settled on Raina's. "All right, before you blow your top. Let me explain."

"Oh, please do."

"Here's your water and diet cola." The waitress returned with their drinks and set them on the table. "Would you like to order?"

Raina took her eyes off Summer for the merest of seconds to glance up and say, "I'll have the Chinese chicken salad." She handed the waitress the menu.

"And I'll have the quinoa and arugula salad," Summer said.

Raina frowned at Summer's healthy choice. Ever since Ryan had gotten on a health-conscious kick, her best friend had stuck to tofu and quinoa in her meals; she was fast becoming not much fun to eat out with.

"I'll get those salads right in for you." Seconds later the waitress was gone and it was just the two of them again.

"I'm waiting—" Raina pointed to her watch "—for that explanation."

"Well…" Summer paused. "When I booked the reservation, it didn't register that it was Spencer's company." She noticed Raina's brow furrow, but she continued, "His assistant mentioned none of this when she booked. It wasn't until I received the deposit check to hold the date that I realized Davis Sports Agency meant Spencer Davis."

"So why didn't you cancel?"

Summer sighed. "That would be unprofessional after I'd accepted."

Raina shook her head in disgust. Spencer knew what he was up to when he'd had his assistant approach their catering service. If she backed out now, she would seem childish, like she couldn't handle being in his company, not to mention that Summer was right. It was bad business to cancel at this late a date. Spencer had painted her into a corner and now they would have cater his event, at his home.

"Please don't be upset with me," Summer pleaded.

"I'm not upset, Summer," Raina responded. "How can I be when you've been taking care of things for months? It's not your fault I have a conflict of interest. I'll just have to make this work."

"Are you sure that's possible?" Summer asked. "After sleeping with the man? I mean you can't go back to acting as if you're immune to him."

"I sure can," Raina said emphatically.

"Why would you want to?" Summer inquired. "You're free. He's free. Why not indulge? Just keep it light."

"Because…I have Zoe. If things don't work out between Spencer and me, imagine how awkward it would be between us."

"You mean like it is now?" Summer asked. "With you trying to avoid the man you've had mad passionate sex with? That's pretty awkward."

"Summer!" Raina was exasperated.

"I speak the truth and you know it," she said. "Which is why you're so irritated with me. If you just allowed yourself to feel what you want instead of stifling your emotions, you'd be better off."

"Whatever."

The waitress came back with their salads. "Can I get you anything else?"

"We're good." Summer spoke up first.

Raina wasn't ready to look in the mirror that Summer was trying to hold up in front of her. She needed to put the feelings that Spencer had stirred up in her back in the closet. There was too much at stake and not just her heart.

"Are you going to speak to me?" Summer asked. "Or are we going to eat in silence? If so I can take this salad to go and eat it at the shop while I prep."

Raina sighed. She could never stay mad at Summer. She appreciated that her best friend spoke her mind while she was usually plagued by self-doubt. "Of course I'm going to talk to you," she replied. "I may not agree with what you have to say, but you have the right to say it."

"How very democratic of you." Summer reached for her water with lemon and sipped generously.

"So what are we going to serve Mr. Davis?" Raina asked.

"You," Summer said with a straight face.

Raina nearly choked on her salad and started coughing furiously. Trust Summer to lighten the tension in the air. Funny part about it was, she was probably right. Spencer probably saw her company handling this event as a way to get closer to her. But he was dead wrong. She was more determined than ever to steer clear of him because if she didn't, Raina feared she would lose her heart.

Chapter 10

"We're not in Kansas anymore," Summer said when they arrived at Spencer's mansion, which boasted a four-car garage, on Star Island, where all the rich and famous in Miami lived.

His home was impressive and his assistant wasted no time telling them the details when she opened the door. "Come in, ladies. I've been waiting for you." Mona ushered them into the foyer that led to an indoor garden and cascading waterfall. "I see you were admiring the exterior. It's custom handcrafted stone."

Raina glanced around. She was used to opulence. This was more understated, yet equally elegant. She glanced up at the leather-clad staircase and forty-foot ceiling that she was sure led to Spencer's master bedroom and swallowed.

"This home is ten thousand square feet, has five

bedrooms and six and a half baths," Mona gushed as she gave them a brief tour of the downstairs. They went past some type of lounging room that housed a big mattress on a center concrete block with lots of throw pillows, past a family area complete with a ten-foot screen and bookshelves, past the billiards and movie rooms until they came to another lounging area with all-white leather furniture and a freestanding bar completely stocked with liquor that reached the ceiling and merged with the custom kitchen.

Raina and Summer both gawked. The kitchen had dark maple cabinets, marble countertops, refrigerators on each side of a built-in wine cooler and two built-in convection ovens. A large island stood in the center with two gas stoves and an extra sink even though there was a double sink against the glass windows that faced the terrace and the infinity pool with a view of the bay. The kitchen was so huge; they could each work a side of the island and never feel cramped.

Summer bumped her hip and Raina finally said, "It's lovely, but we'd better get to work."

"Let me know if you need anything," Mona replied.

"And Mr. Davis?" Raina almost held her breath when she asked.

Mona smiled warmly. "Oh, don't you worry, Ms. Martin. I'll be your main contact for the evening."

Raina could only manage a nod and Summer said, "Of course. Thank you for the tour."

After she'd gone, Raina finally released the breath she'd been holding. She'd psyched herself out so much about this dinner that her stomach had been in knots all morning. She was sure Spencer had set this event up to get close to her, so why was he hiding behind his assistant? And what was his end game?

Spencer nervously paced the bedroom of his mansion. He'd showered over an hour ago, donned trousers and a royal-blue dress shirt and was ready for the evening to start, but he hadn't yet left his room.

Raina and her catering team were downstairs in his kitchen at this very minute preparing for his client appreciation party. He knew he had to play it cool tonight and act like he'd only hired Raina because her company was one of the best in Miami and not because he hoped to spend some precious alone time with the woman who'd thoroughly captivated his attention from the moment he'd seen her standing behind the chef's table at Allyson Peters's party.

He'd made sure Mona was organizing the party, thereby showing Raina that they could share a professional working relationship even though he wanted more. A lot more. The one night he'd spent with Raina had meant more to him than any other experience he'd had with a woman. He hadn't just been enjoying her body on a primitive level; he'd been connecting with her soul. He felt as if he was coming to understand her and she him.

But Raina was still shutting him out. Since he'd overheard Zoe at the basketball game saying she wished she had a father, Raina had been even more distant. He'd called several times to just speak to Zoe, but she either hadn't picked up or had told him Zoe wasn't there. She couldn't avoid him forever. It was high time she faced him and the fact that he wasn't going anywhere.

He was hoping he would not have to get attorneys

involved, but if she persisted in avoiding him and deny-ing him access to his niece, he was going to have to take drastic measures. Spencer went to his nightstand drawer and grabbed a foil packet and placed it in his pocket.

After he was sure a sufficient amount of time had passed and a fair number of guests had arrived, Spen-cer took a deep breath and left the room. *Let the party begin.*

"Soup's ready," Raina called. "We need to hustle and get them plated before they get cold." She slapped her hands together to get the servers' attention. "Chop-chop."

"I think we all get it," Summer said as she helped plate the warm mushroom salad she was serving.

"Sorry," Raina replied, eyeing her partner.

Summer came toward her and whispered, "Relax" in Raina's ear so only she could hear.

"I'll try." Raina was on edge. She hadn't yet seen the man of the house. He was making himself scarce, which surprised her. She'd thought since he'd gone through the effort of procuring her services that he would be on hand to oversee the event. Far from it. Mona was cracking the whip and making sure everyone from the caterer to the DJ to the photographer was on schedule.

Raina didn't know what made her more nervous, that she hadn't seen Spencer or that she would. She knew he couldn't be pleased with her. Ever since they'd at-tended the basketball game, she'd kept her distance and it hadn't gone unnoticed. Even Zoe had commented yesterday that it had been nearly a week since they'd seen Spence. She'd wondered aloud if he was starting to forget about them when he promised he'd come around more.

Raina felt terrible for keeping Zoe from him, but she knew she didn't have time on her side. If she and Spencer didn't come to a resolution and soon about Zoe, he would take her to court. She just wasn't sure she could handle Spencer becoming a fixture in her life. Whenever he was around, she felt out of control and acted impulsively. It was like she didn't have any willpower and knowing he held that kind of power over her really scared her.

At just that moment, Spencer and Mona walked into the kitchen. A knot formed in Raina's stomach and she tried to erect a wall of defense against the potency of Spencer's maleness, but it was futile. He looked scrumptious. "Good evening, ladies." Spencer smiled warmly at Summer first before resting his dark eyes on Raina after they'd traveled over her body.

"Mr. Davis." Summer and Raina spoke almost simultaneously.

"Ms. Newman. Ms. Martin." Spencer nodded curtly as he walked toward her. "Do you have anything I can taste?"

"We sure do," Raina replied, a little too excitedly for her liking. "I have this delicious curried butternut squash soup. We put it in a shot glass for ease."

Raina handed Spencer a shot glass and when he grasped it, his hands made a point of coming into contact with hers. His eyes raked hers for what seemed like an eternity before he let go.

Spencer put the glass to those sensuous thick lips of his, lips that had stroked her into orgasm after orgasm, and Raina's insides instantly lurched with excitement at the memory.

"Delicious." Spencer licked his lips as he placed the glass on counter. "I'm sure the rest of the meal will be equally delicious. I'll see you both soon." He nodded at Raina and Summer again before leaving the kitchen.

Raina was rooted to the spot and Summer called her out on it.

"Hello." Summer waved her hand in front of Raina's face.

Raina blinked several times. "What?" she asked, annoyed.

"What?" Summer stepped backward. "The sexual tension was spilling off the both of you in droves. When he licked his lips, I thought you might expire. Poor Mona and I felt like we were intruding."

"That's ridiculous." Raina moved away to the sink to rinse off some vegetables for her duck breast.

"You can deny it if you want," Summer said. "But things between you two are far from over. In fact, I think they are just getting started."

Embarrassed, Raina kept her back to her friend, not because Summer was wrong, but because she knew she was right. If she could see it, feel it, just how long would Raina be able to keep her feelings for Spencer at bay?

The rest of the evening continued smoothly and without event. Periodically, Spencer stopped in the kitchen to have a taste of the next course. He particularly seemed to enjoy her pan-seared duck breast with plum reduction. And he just about licked the plate when he tasted their bourbon bananas Foster.

Each time Spencer came to the kitchen, it became easier and easier, and slowly Raina began to relax and enjoy cooking like she usually did without the anxiety of wondering what his next move was going to be.

By the time dessert was over and the guests were enjoying coffee and brandy, Raina and Summer finally took the time to have a seat and have a drink to the evening's success. They'd already packed up all the food and now it was just a matter of cleanup, especially now that most guests had departed.

"Great job, partner." Summer clicked the champagne flute she'd procured from one of the servers against Raina's, then set it down on the counter bar.

"Back at you," Raina replied, taking a seat beside her. "We make a great team."

"Always have," Summer said, sipping her drink. "And now that we're doing so well, we should start enjoying the fruits of our labor. You know, take some time for ourselves."

"We can't back off now. We're hot. Did you see how many guests asked for our cards?" Raina pointed with her flute toward the lounging area. "They loved our food."

"True, but there has to be room in our lives for more than just this business."

Raina frowned. She didn't like where this conversation was going. "Like what?"

"Like that fine man in there." Summer pointed to the lounge. "There's no reason you two can't explore a relationship."

Raina put down her flute and jumped off her bar stool. "That's not possible."

"Why is that?" a masculine voice said from behind her.

Raina closed her eyes and wished the floor would

swallow her up whole. How long had he been standing there? He had a habit of eavesdropping.

Raina opened her eyes and watched Summer rise from the bar. "Um, we should really start to clean up."

"Leave it!" Spencer ordered.

"Mr. Davis—" Summer began, but Spencer must have given her a look. Raina had never seen Summer cower before.

"Summer, I think it's fine for you to leave now. Don't you think?"

Summer looked at Raina and although her eyes were downcast, Raina nodded her agreement. Reluctantly, Summer grabbed her purse from underneath the island counter and left the room.

Slowly Raina turned around and lifted her eyes to meet Spencer's. "You really shouldn't boss people around like that." She attempted to sound light, but it came off somewhat forced.

Spencer didn't speak; he just rolled up his sleeves, headed to the sink and began washing dishes. Raina had expected a fight and didn't know how to react. She stood there woodenly until he glanced at her and said, "You wanna help?"

"Oh, yes, I'm sorry," Raina said and sidled next to him. She helped rinse off the dishes he'd washed and set them on a rack to dry. "I'm sure you have staff that could do this for you," she commented.

"I do," he said but didn't offer further explanation and continued scrubbing the pots and pans.

Raina wondered when they were going to have it out and the waiting was driving her crazy. She'd expected the Spencer who'd come into the shower and ravished her on the bathroom floor. She wasn't expecting this calm and cool Spencer, and it unnerved her. Was he purposely trying to keep her off-kilter?

Spencer regarded Raina when she wasn't looking. She'd anticipated that he would act caveman and come on strong, but this time he was actually trying to heed Ty's advice. He was going to try talking to her calmly and rationally about the future.

When he was finished with the last pot, he handed it to her, rinsed off the sink and wiped down the counters. He turned to lean back against the counter as she put away the remaining dishes.

"Would you like a drink?" he asked.

"I have one." She motioned to the glass of champagne on the counter.

"I meant a real drink. A glass of brandy, perhaps?" He walked over to a cabinet and reached inside to produce two tumblers.

"I suppose that would be fine," she said, taking a seat at the island. She removed her apron and set it on the counter.

He hoped so. Brandy had a tendency to relax people, and he needed Raina relaxed and unguarded. He walked over to the bar in the adjacent room and poured two generous glasses. He returned to the kitchen and handed Raina one.

"You did a great job on the party," Spencer stated, taking a sip of his brandy and leaning against the counter opposite Raina.

"Are we really going to make small talk?" Raina asked. "I doubt that's why you sent my ride home. Why don't we just get to the heart of the matter?"

That was fine with him. Spencer was ready to face

the situation head-on, but he wanted to do so with a modicum of decorum. "All right," he said and sauntered toward her.

Spencer came to stand in front of Raina, getting closer until they were inches apart. "So why don't you tell me why you and I won't work."

"Why don't you tell me why we would?" Raina countered.

"Let's not play games, Raina."

"I'm not," she replied. "You're a rich former NBA star turned sports agent with women lined up at your door. Why would I knowingly walk into that scenario?"

Spencer nodded his head. So she wanted to use his playboy reputation as an excuse. *Fine.* He intended to knock down every excuse she put in their path. "Have you seen me with any women recently? Or photographed with any women?"

"No, but that means nothing. Athletes are known to hide their women. You wouldn't be the first."

"True, but I don't want any other women, Raina," he whispered. "Just you."

"You want what you can't have because it's new and different, but as soon as the newness wears off you'll be on to the next new plaything. I won't be your latest woman du jour."

Spencer slapped his glass down on the counter so hard that some liquid spilled on the counter. "Ah, so I'm just a playboy looking to use you for a good time? Is that really how you see me?" He'd hoped in the short time that they'd known each other that she thought better of him.

"I don't know you," Raina said. At his frown, she

rephrased. "At least not well enough to form any real opinion."

"Have I done anything that would make you not trust me?" Spencer inquired. Raina's silence told him he was making some headway. "I've been open and honest with you about what I want, haven't I?" He took her brandy tumbler out of her hand and placed it on the island, using his other hand to cup her backside and pull her off the stool and bring her toward him. "But you keep resisting me." He stroked her cheek. "Why do you keep fighting me, fighting yourself?" He leaned down and brushed a soft kiss across the tender spot at the nape of Raina's neck.

"You're not playing fair," she murmured against him.

"I know," he said, suckling her neck and then moving up to lick her earlobes and blow warm air on her dampened skin. "I want you to give in to me." He rubbed the thickness of his erection against her center and began massaging one of her breasts through the cotton T-shirt she wore.

"I can't," Raina whispered.

"Yes, you can," he murmured. He didn't wait for a response. Grabbing her by the buttocks, he lifted her in the air and sat her down on the island counter. There was no more time for decorum. There was only time for action. He yanked the T-shirt over her head, leaving her in only a satin bra and jeans. His mouth chartered every inch of her lips, slowly and leisurely, before his tongue finally pressed for entry inside her mouth. She parted her lips, and his tongue thrust inside her mouth and tangled with hers. He groped for the zipper on her jeans as he made love to her with his mouth.

Then he moved back ever so slightly so he could pull

the jeans from her long, lean legs. He tossed them to the kitchen floor. He kneed her legs apart and settled between them. His mouth slid down her neck and his took a teasing bite at the spot on her neck that joined her shoulders before arriving to her breasts. He pushed aside the satiny fabric of her bra and lowered his head to her naked breasts.

Raina held his head in her hands as he used his tongue to roll and lick one breast and then the other until they became erect underneath his expert mouth. Raina began to moan and shift on the counter as he sucked her breasts like they were exotic pieces of ripe fruit.

Spencer was eager for more and moved his hot hands lower until they came into contact with the satin of her briefs. He pushed the tiny scrap aside so his fingers could tease her already slick feminine folds. She was wet for him and her clit was firm. She opened up wider for him as his fingers guided their way in and out of her moist petals. When she began to twitch, Spencer knew he wanted nothing more than to taste her sweet nectar. In seconds, he'd lowered himself to his knees and replaced his fingers with his tongue. He held her hips in a strong clutch and tongued her until she was on fire, breathing deeply, moaning, twitching, begging him to enter her.

"Spencer…" she said through ragged breaths. "Please…"

"Tell me you need this as much as I do," he rasped against her feverish thighs, looking up at her.

"I need you…"

Spencer lifted his head, rose to his feet and kissed her neck while Raina swiftly tore at the buttons of his shirt, sending several flying through the air. The buckle of his belt was next, and his pants fell to the floor while he fumbled putting on a condom.

Raina scooted forward on the counter and wrapped her legs around Spencer. He pushed aside the tiny strap of satin again to plunge deep inside her. Her fingers dug into his naked backside as Spencer closed his eyes and began pumping into her. She didn't know it, but she owned him. He'd never met a woman who could give herself so freely to him as Raina did. He thrust inside her urgently and she met each of his thrusts until his pace began to both sate and exhaust him.

When neither of them could take any more he gave one final thrust. Raina cried out softly, but he muffled her cries by covering her mouth with his. Small eruptions happened inside his body unlike anything he'd ever encountered. He wrestled with it at first and then eventually gave himself up to the pleasure and sank against her as her head fell back against the granite.

Several moments passed before Spencer eventually disengaged himself from Raina and reached down to pull his pants up. He started to button his shirt, then realized several buttons had popped off in their hasty union. He'd been so eager to be inside her that he hadn't even taken Raina to his bedroom and made love to her properly like he'd intended. Instead, he'd just taken her like a horny schoolboy right there on the kitchen counter.

Where had his calm gone? Ty's words had certainly flown out the window. But had they made any progress? He doubted it. All he'd done was make her crazy with sex. And, yes, Raina understood the intensity of their passion, even shared it, but was that enough to show her they could have a future together? A future with Zoe?

Raina slowly rose from the counter. He could see she was embarrassed as she glanced down for the jeans he'd discarded earlier in a hurry.

"Raina…"

"God, what are you doing to me?" Raina said, slipping into her jeans and zipping them up. "And why do we keep ending up here?"

He wasn't sure if she was speaking to him or thinking out loud. "Was that a rhetorical question?"

She turned to glare at him. "I…I've never been this… this woman before…so, so wanton for sex with no regard for when or where. You are a bad influence." She pointed at him. "It's exactly why I need to keep my distance. I have no self-control. No filter when it comes to you."

"And that's a bad thing?" he asked.

"I like to be in control. I have to know what's coming."

"I know."

"Don't patronize me."

"I'm not," Spencer responded. "But you can't control everything, Raina. You can't control this…us." He motioned to the two of them.

"So you keep showing me," Raina said tartly.

"What are you so afraid of?" Spencer asked. "Why do you keep running away from me? Don't you see that I want to be with you?"

"I…I…" Raina glanced around for her shirt.

Spencer saw it lying near the table nearby and he blocked her path as she tried to move past him. "Stay with me tonight, Raina," he pleaded, bracing his arms against hers. "I promise you it won't be like before. Give me a chance to show you how good it could be between us. How soft and gentle I can be again." He caressed her cheek with the palm of his hand.

"Spencer...don't do this to me," Raina murmured in a low, throaty voice. Her words said she wanted to leave, but her body hadn't moved a muscle.

"Please, Raina," he said.

When she didn't utter another protest, he lifted her into his arms, walked through the foyer and carried her up the stairs to his bedroom.

Chapter 11

Hours later after Spencer made love to her slowly and reverently, they'd fallen asleep in each other's arms. Raina awoke and it was still dark out, which meant she hadn't been asleep long. At first she was disconcerted and she thought it was because she wasn't used to sleeping in a stranger's bed, but then she realized that wasn't what had woken her up.

Spencer was thrashing around on the huge king-size bed and calling out his brother's name in his sleep. He seemed to be in the throes of some of kind nightmare.

"Spencer…" Raina reached out to touch him and Spencer shot straight up and glared at her. "Spencer!"

He blinked several times as if he was trying to focus on her before shaking his head and snapping out of the nightmare. "Are you okay?" he finally asked.

"I am," Raina replied. "But I don't think you are."

She touched his chest, which was damp with perspiration. "You were screaming out Cameron's name."

"Oh, that," Spencer said as he pushed up several pillows so he could lean back on them. "That's nothing."

"Nothing?" Raina asked incredulously. "I don't think so. You were yelling out his name. Wait a second." She paused as she watched him. "You've had this nightmare before, haven't you?"

Spencer nodded.

"For how long?"

"Years. Since the accident."

"Years?" Raina was dumbfounded. How could he go on having the same nightmare? "Have you talked to anyone about it?"

"I've been shrinked to death," Spencer replied glumly. "And seeing them hasn't stopped the nightmares from occurring. It seems that they've gotten worse, especially of late."

"It's because of Zoe, isn't it? Finding out about her has stirred up all those emotions." Raina took a stab in the dark at the root cause.

Spencer shrugged. "Perhaps, perhaps not."

"Do you want to talk about it?" Raina asked.

"Not particularly."

Raina was sure he didn't want to appear weak, but for Raina it was the exact opposite. It showed her that Spencer was human like the rest of them despite his aura of confidence and strength. It made him more approachable, like when she'd learned about his mother.

Raina reached across to slide her small hand into his large one. "Do you feel guilty for surviving the accident?"

Spencer sighed loudly and then jerked away and rose

from the bed. Clearly he didn't want to talk about it, and he probably didn't appreciate Raina pressing him for more information. He walked over to the window and stared out, oblivious to his gloriously perfect naked body.

Raina tried not to stare at the hard chiseled lines of his stomach or his firm buttocks in the moonlight coming through the sheer curtains that led out onto a balcony.

He was quiet for several moments, and she waited until he finally spoke. "I do feel guilty. Cameron was my little brother and I was supposed to look out for him and ensure he didn't get hurt. You see, that was my place in life," he said, turning around to face her. She couldn't see his eyes, but she knew he was crying. "To take care of Cam after Mom and Dad died. And I didn't."

"He was a grown man," Raina responded. "And responsible for his own actions."

"I know that, here." Spencer pointed to his head. "But tell that to my heart, a heart that yearns for my... my little brother."

"You have to forgive yourself for whatever you think you should have done."

"I was driving!" he yelled. "I made sure he didn't get behind the wheel, but I didn't make sure he was wearing a seat belt. How could I have been so stupid? If he'd just been wearing a seat belt, he would have survived.... He wouldn't have gone fl-flying through that...that window. The image of his body...bruised... bloodied... It haunts me, Raina."

Swiftly, she rose and crossed the room in seconds to wrap her arms around Spencer's middle. "It's not your fault," she cried.

"Yes, it is," Spencer murmured, bending his head and crying into her hair as she held him. "I didn't protect him."

"Listen to me." She looked up at him with tearstained cheeks and her eyes glistening. "You have to forgive yourself. You did the best you could. You didn't let him drive drunk. Just think about it—if he'd been driving drunk, he could have killed himself and other people."

"Instead I killed him."

"You didn't kill your brother." Both of Raina's hands clasped Spencer's face. "It was an accident. You hear me? It was an accident. You couldn't control it any more than we could control the fact that my sister died of cancer at twenty-eight. But she did. And all you can do is go on living, Spencer."

"It's just so hard sometimes."

Raina nodded in agreement. "Trust me, I know. But Cameron wouldn't want you to keep blaming yourself. He'd want you to live life to the fullest because, as we know, tomorrow isn't promised."

Her words seemed to penetrate through Spencer's thick skull, because he said, "Does that mean you're going to live those same words?"

"What do you mean?"

"It means are you going to live life to the fullest? Are you going to allow yourself to be happy?"

Raina smiled up at him. "With you?"

Spencer tugged her closer to him. "Yeah, with me. You have any other six-foot-four former basketball stars in mind?"

"I don't." Raina chuckled. "But then again it seems we Martin women have a thing for b-ball players."

"Don't you even joke like that," Spencer said. "You're mine, woman."

"Yours?" No one had ever claimed her as theirs before. Most times she thought her family acted as if she didn't exist or was a cross they had to bear.

"Yes, mine." He lifted her into his arms again and walked back to the bed. "And I don't intend on letting you go." He laid her gently down and then joined her, the full weight of his frame causing the mattress to sink lower.

"You'll have to let me go in the morning," Raina said. She had to go pick up Zoe and start their weekend routine of birthday parties and recitals. "I have another little person to look after." Thankfully her parents were watching Zoe, which was why she hadn't minded when Summer had departed with the company van.

"But that's much later," Spencer said. He wrapped his arms around her shoulders and pulled her into his arms and covered her mouth with his.

The next morning, Spencer convinced her to leave Zoe in her parents' care for one more day and they'd spent most of Saturday together. Not only in bed, but getting to know each other. They'd gone jogging on the beach and then come back, showered and made love again before finally going out to dinner. Eventually they'd talked about Zoe. Spencer hadn't come on as strong as before.

He indicated he wanted to spend time with Zoe and get to know his niece, and Raina had agreed she wouldn't stand in his way anymore. The conversation hadn't gotten beyond Spencer visiting; but Raina was sure that if she gave Spencer more access to Zoe, he would see that she was in good hands under Raina's care.

* * *

Raina knew her parents were not going to be happy, but she'd invited Spencer to come trick-or-treating with her and Zoe in her parents' neighborhood on Halloween. Her parents were of the opinion that Spencer had no place in their lives, but Raina was starting to believe otherwise. Spencer rang the doorbell several days later and Raina's heart began beating in her chest at the thought of seeing him again. "Come on in," Raina said, opening the door with a flourish.

"Wow!" Spencer's eyes widened at Raina's getup. She'd taken the liberty of going to the costume store and picking out a Black Widow superhero costume complete with black spandex jumpsuit, adorned belt, leg straps and wrist cuffs. The jumpsuit was skintight and hugged every curve and showed off her butt. The swell of her breasts peeked out from the V of the jumpsuit.

"You look great, too." She laughed, walking him into the foyer.

Spencer must have had the same idea because he'd gotten into Halloween and was dressed as Thor with a red cape and fake hammer. The fake muscles molded into the arms and torso of the costume weren't necessary because Spencer could easily fill it out on his own. Raina knew intimately well just how chiseled his body was. She smiled at the knowledge.

"Where is our witch?" he asked, looking around.

"She's upstairs putting the finishing touches on her costume."

Spencer smiled. "Good. That gives us a few minutes alone." He led her into the darkened living room.

"Spencer, what if Zoe—" But she never got the words out because he pressed her up against a wall and gave her a deliciously sinful kiss that reminded her of all the things he would do to her when they were alone later.

Eventually, he lifted his head and stared down at her. "I can't wait to have you," he whispered huskily.

"And I can't wait to be had." She chuckled mischievously.

"Auntie Raina, was that Spence?" She heard the pitter-patter of light footsteps as Zoe made her way down the stairs. She found them in the living room.

"What are you guys doing in the dark?" Zoe asked, turning on the lamp on a nearby side table.

"Oh, nothing." Raina gave Spencer a knowing wink and came forward to greet her. "Don't you look like the prettiest witch ever?"

Her niece had dressed in a black-and-purple peasant dress with full moon appliqué, witch's hat and black tights with shiny boots.

Zoe's eyes grew bright. "Do you really think so?" she asked enthusiastically.

"But of course," Spencer said. "You can help me protect earth from those crazy witches."

Zoe gave a hearty belly laugh. "Spence, there's no witches in the Thor movie."

"What do you think of my costume?" Spence asked Zoe, spinning around to give Zoe a full view.

"Not as good as mine, but you'll do." She smiled.

They all began laughing as they headed out the door.

Spencer, Raina and Zoe shared a great evening in her parents' neighborhood trick-or-treating. Most people thought they were together and commented that they made a beautiful family. Raina wasn't sure if she was ready or could ever see herself as part of a family since she'd always felt like an outcast in her own, but she played along.

Alexa had always been the apple of her parents' eyes and she could do no wrong. Instead of being angry that her parents favored her twin, Raina had cherished her even more. Halloween had always been one of their favorite holidays.

"You okay?" Spencer asked, tapping into her thoughts as she stood back and allowed Zoe to ring the doorbell at a neighbor's home.

Raina nodded. "I'm fine. I was just thinking about me and Alexa."

"You were close?"

"Yes, like you and Cameron, I assume?" Raina replied, giving Spencer a sideward glance.

"Then you must miss her as much as I miss him."

Raina turned to watch Zoe return with an ever-increasing sack of candy that she was finding hard to carry. "Even more so when I see her walking back to me." She reached for Zoe's sack. "Here, let me carry that."

Zoe swatted away her hand. "I've got it, Auntie Raina."

Raina laughed. "I'm not going to take your candy away. But that bag is starting to get as big as you."

"I know." Zoe's eyes grew large with excitement. "I can't wait to eat it all."

"You can have a few pieces tonight before bed," Raina replied. "But now it's time to head back to Grandma and Grandpa's and say good-night."

"But…" Zoe folded her arms across her chest as if to pout.

"You can have some more candy tomorrow," Raina added. "But it's late. We need to be heading home."

Zoe didn't speak; she just stalked ahead of Raina and Spencer toward her grandparents' home.

"She's real feisty, isn't she?" Spencer asked. He fell into a slower pace to keep up with Raina's shorter strides.

"She's a little woman," Raina said. "And very opinionated."

"Not unlike someone else I know."

Raina turned and frowned at Spencer, but as soon as he began laughing, her frown turned into a smile.

"Truth hurts, doesn't it?" He chuckled just as they approached her parents' home.

Her mother must have been looking out the window because as soon as they started climbing the stairs, the front door swung open and Crystal rushed out the door.

"How was trick-or-treating?" she asked Zoe.

"I got chocolate and lollipops and a whole lot more," Zoe said excitedly.

Her mother turned to give Spencer a long glare before ushering Zoe inside to hear the details, leaving Spencer and Raina on the front porch outside.

"Wow! Your mom doesn't like me much," Spencer said. Instead of following them inside, he chose to sit down on the swing on the porch.

"It's not personal," Raina said, joining him on the swing. When she saw his wrinkled brow, she revised her statement. "Okay it is personal. She sees your presence as a threat and that you could take Zoe away from us."

"Why would she think that?"

"Because it's probably what she would do," Raina

answered honestly. "If she had custody, she would forbid you to see Zoe."

"Well, I'm glad that's not the case." Spencer brought one of Raina's hands to his lips. "I'm glad you see the value of having me in Zoe's life." Then he leaned over to press his lips to hers. They coaxed hers apart until she opened her mouth and allowed him access. He stroked her tongue with his and set Raina ablaze with passion.

"Ahem, ahem."

Raina turned to see her father standing beside the swing. He had an odd look on his face. If Raina didn't know any better, she would have sworn it was disappointment. But it swiftly disappeared and he said, "Uh, would you like to come in for some hot cocoa before you leave?"

"Would love some," Spencer said, swiftly rising to his feet and helping Raina up.

Raina objected, "Sorry, Dad, we really need to get going. It is a school night."

"One cup," her father said.

Raina sighed. "All right." They followed him inside and began heading to the kitchen, but her father stopped Raina.

"You go on ahead, Mr. Davis. I need to speak with my daughter for a moment."

Spencer's gaze penetrated Raina's, asking her whether he should stay, but she implored him with her eyes to go.

"A word, Raina." Anthony motioned for her to precede him.

She knew where they were going, the study. The infamous place he used to take Alexa and Raina whenever they'd been in trouble.

Once the study door closed, Raina said, "Okay, Dad. Let's hear it."

"Do you really think it's wise getting romantically involved with that man?"

"Daddy—" she began, but he held up his hand to stop her.

"That man is a seducer just like his brother. They're athletes. They are used to having a woman at their side. I don't want you to get used and tossed aside like his brother did to Alexa. You see what happened to her, she ended up alone and pregnant. And you have Zoe now. You have to make smarter choices."

"That isn't going to happen here," Raina responded. "You don't know Spencer like I do. Just because they are related does not mean he's anything like his brother."

"You saw the press the attorney dug up on him."

"That was four years ago, Dad. He's different after losing his brother. He changed his whole life."

"I hope for your sake that's the case, baby girl," Anthony said and pulled her toward him into a big bear hug. "Because I'd hate to see you heartbroken," he said the words against her hair. "Not to mention, his getting close to you could be just a way for him to get dirt for his custody case."

Raina pulled back to look up at him. "He's said nothing about that. It's a moot point."

"Do you really believe that?"

"I do," she said, stepping out of his embrace. But even as said she said the words, a smidgen of doubt swirled through her. Could her father be right? Could Spencer be setting her up for a fall? She shook her head. No, no, no, she refused to believe it. "I do," she said more emphatically.

Her father shrugged. "All right, then. Let's go check on the gang."

Raina found Spencer sitting at the kitchen table with her mother and Zoe. Crystal was ignoring Spencer, while Zoe held court talking to the both of them.

"Where's that hot chocolate I was promised?" Raina tried to sound upbeat to ease the tension in the room.

A few minutes later, she was holding a mug of steaming cocoa in her hands, "Thanks, Mom."

"I'm so glad you're here, Spence." Zoe smiled up adoringly at Spencer.

"I'm glad I could be here." Spencer caressed Zoe's hair.

Raina saw the gut-wrenching look pass between her mother and father. It was hard not to. She didn't know how to make the situation better and get her parents to realize that Spencer wasn't a threat unless they made him one. Would she ever be able to convince them?

Chapter 12

Once they made it back to Raina's house and had put a hyped-on-sugar Zoe to bed, Raina and Spencer sat listening to jazz as they drank wine on her living room floor. They were still in costume, though Spencer had removed his Thor cape and Raina had removed her sexy black four-inch-heeled boots. Raina couldn't remember the last time she'd felt this comfortable with a man. Being with Spencer was so easy it scared her. *Is it possible to be this happy?*

"What's on your mind?" Spencer asked.

"Me…you…this."

"You're wondering if it's real."

When Raina nodded, Spencer slid over and wrapped his arms around her. "It's real, Raina. Why do you find it so hard to believe that?"

"A lifetime of always being in the shadows and learning to never expect anything. Only what I could create."

"With your parents?" he inquired intuitively.

She turned and looked up at him. "Why would you ask that?"

"Because I see how they dote on Zoe. And if they are as overbearing with her, then it stands to reason they could have been the same way with…Alexa, perhaps? Leaving you to wonder what was wrong with you and why you weren't so special?"

Raina nodded but didn't look at him. "You hit the nail on the head."

He grasped her head and forced her to look up at him. Her eyes were bordered with tears. "You're special to *me,* Raina. Can't you see how hard I've fallen for you?"

His head slowly descended until his lips met hers. His kiss was light as a summer breeze, but Raina quivered nonetheless at the sweet tenderness of his kiss.

"Make love to me," she said.

Spencer rose from the floor and held out his hand to pull Raina to her feet. He kept her hand in his as he led her upstairs to her bedroom.

Once they were behind closed doors, Raina found two candles and lit them, casting the room in a shadowy light while Spencer began to remove his cumbersome Thor costume. When the candles were all lit, Raina met him back at her queen-size bed.

Spencer was laid out against her pillows, wearing only his boxer briefs. A three-pack of condoms was lying nearby; they knew they would need all of them. He sat watching her as she made her way to the side of the bed and began to undress for him. She started by removing the wrist cuffs, leg straps and belt buckle and dropping them to the floor.

Spencer smiled as she continued her striptease. When she reached the zipper at her bust, she slowly slid it down her abdomen until it stopped at her waist. Then she bent down so she could slide out of the jumpsuit one leg at a time.

There was no denying the lust in Spencer's dark eyes, but she had some of her own that she wanted to work out. When she was down to her bra and G-string, she unlatched the snap of her bra and the strap of satin fell unceremoniously to the floor. Her G-string followed suit, and she was standing naked in front of him.

"You're beautiful," Spencer whispered and held out his hand to her. "Come here."

She joined him on the bed. Instead of letting him take charge, she bent her head and licked his nipples, teasing them with her tongue until they became hard peaks. She continued a path to his navel and his lower abdomen; she heard his sharp intake of breath as her fingers closed around the band of his briefs and eased them down his muscled thighs and legs. When he was as naked as she, she gave him a wicked smile and closed one hand around his burgeoning erection. She licked the tip of his penis at first and then sucked the tip, teasing Spencer until his breathing thickened. Spencer took her head in his hands and her mouth moved up and down his hard length to the rhythm he needed.

"Oh, yes, Raina, like that," he moaned. Raina took him deeper inside her mouth again and again.

When she was sure he was hard and ready for her, she reached for a foil packet, removed a condom and placed it on his erect penis, protecting them both. Then she swung both legs around his waist and began to ride him. She rolled her hips forward and backward, forming a steady rhythm that had Spencer moaning softly.

"Oh, God, Raina," Spencer groaned underneath her.

Raina changed techniques and squatted on him, bouncing up and down and taking him deeper and deeper inside her body. It felt so good for him to be inside her, and Raina relished that she could bring him such joy.

When it seemed he could take no more, Spencer grabbed her by the hips and flipped her on her back until she was underneath him and he was in control. He thrust deep inside until he found her spot. Then he sucked her already erect nipples. Although her breasts felt huge, Spencer made them feel beautiful as he cupped them in his hands. But he didn't stop there, his hips continued to circle hers, massaging the spot first with his erect penis and then with his fingers until Raina's orgasm hit her like a ton of bricks and she whimpered her release.

"Spencer…"

Spencer's lips reached for hers once more so he could continue the dance with soft kisses, moans and thrusts before he too succumbed to wave after wave of the never-ending pleasure that had enveloped Raina.

Spencer awoke the next morning in Raina's arms. Although there was no place he'd rather be, he hadn't meant to sleep over. He'd intended on sneaking out in the middle of the night, but last night Raina had taken charge. She'd ridden him until he was moaning, shuddering and trembling as ripples after ripples of orgasm ran through his body like the aftershocks of an earth-quake.

He glanced at the alarm clock on Raina's nightstand: it read 7:00 a.m. He was sure Zoe had to be getting up soon for school. So, if he could get dressed and sneak out before she found him in Raina's room, all would be well and the peaceful calm he'd created wouldn't be disturbed.

He slid away from Raina, who was still dead to the world, and went to the bathroom. After freshening up and writing a quick note to Raina and leaving it on her nightstand, Spencer exited her bedroom. He heard a shriek behind him.

"Spence?"

Spencer rolled his eyes upward. He'd been caught. Slowly, he turned around to find Zoe staring at him bug-eyed and wearing cartoon-print pajamas.

"What are you doing here?"

"Uh...uh..." For once in his life, Spencer was at a loss for words. How did he explain to a six-year-old that he'd just spent the night with her aunt?

Thank God he didn't have to, because Raina appeared in her bedroom doorway, dressed in a silk robe. She said, "Zoe, Spence had a sleepover here last night. He—" she gave him a furtive glance "—was too tired to go home."

"So he stayed in your room?" Zoe pressed. "Like other daddies?"

Spencer watched horror spread across Raina's face at Zoe's leaped-to conclusion and before she could an-swer, Zoe was already rushing into his arms. "I'm so happy, Spence." She squeezed his legs. "You and Auntie Raina can get married and we can be a family. This is so awesome!"

He looked down at Zoe and then at Raina and mouthed, "I'm so sorry."

"Zoe." Raina came toward her. "It's time for you to get ready for school. Why don't you get washed up and we'll meet you downstairs?"

Zoe started for the bathroom, but then she spun around. "You'll be here when I get out of the shower?" she asked, looking directly at Spencer.

He stared at Raina. When she nodded, he said, "Okay, sure thing, munchkin."

"Great!" A large grin spread across Zoe's cheeks and she rushed off to the bathroom adjoining her room.

Once he heard running water, Spencer turned to Raina. "I'm sorry, babe. I overslept and I was trying to sneak out and—"

"I'm not upset with you," Raina replied. "She was bound to figure it out sooner rather than later. I was just hoping to have figured out what we were going to tell her before she leaped to conclusions."

"And what are we going to tell her?"

Raina shrugged. "I don't know. I haven't figured that out yet. Care for a cup of coffee?" she asked.

"Sounds great."

Several minutes later, Spencer was seated at Raina's wooden table in her breakfast nook while she busied herself in the kitchen making a pot of coffee. Zoe catching him leaving Raina's bedroom had been unexpected and he was unsure of how to proceed. They were already on soft footing, so he waited for direction from Raina.

Eventually after the coffee started brewing, she took

a seat at the table beside him. "So, I guess we need to explain us to Zoe."

"And how would you characterize us?" Spencer inquired. He sure as hell wasn't certain. Were they dating, committed or just kicking it?

"We tell her the truth," Raina replied as if the truth was obvious to him. "That we like each other a lot and that we'll be spending a lot more time together."

That makes the situation real clear, Spencer thought.

He must have had a look of consternation because Raina clarified, "She's a little girl, Spencer. I don't know how to better explain it than that. I don't want her getting her hopes up that we'll be more than that."

"You mean a family?" Spencer asked. "Isn't that what we are? Heck, we haven't told her I'm her uncle yet. Don't you think it's high time we tell Zoe the truth?"

"Tell me what?" Zoe said from the doorway. She was already dressed for school in jeans and a pink pullover sweater with lots of sparkle and glitter.

Raina rolled her eyes upward, making Spencer wonder if she ever had any intention of telling Zoe his true identity.

Raina shrugged. "Come here, sweetheart," she said, opening her arms wide for Zoe. Zoe sat in her lap. Raina gave her a big squeeze and a kiss. "You know how you said you felt like we were a family?"

"Yes?" Zoe asked, wide-eyed.

"Well, I have some news." Raina brushed Zoe's wayward curls out of her face so she could look at her niece intently. "Spence here is more than Auntie Raina's friend. He's related to you. He's your uncle."

Zoe frowned. "My uncle? But you and Mommy were Grandma's…" Zoe paused midsentence and thought about what Raina had said. She then turned to face Spencer with her big doe eyes. "If Mommy and Auntie Raina were Grandma's only children, then…" She looked at Spencer as if searching for some sign of resemblance. "Then you're my daddy's brother?"

Spencer nodded and he watched as the weight of the information settled on Zoe and more questions formed.

"Where is he then?" she asked, her voice steadily rising. "Where's my daddy?" She looked at Spencer and then at Raina. He could see tears forming as she asked again, "Where's my daddy?"

Raina swallowed. "I'm sorry, baby, but your daddy, Spencer's brother, passed away like your mommy."

"He's dead?" A tear rolled down her cheek.

"Yes," was the sole word Raina could muster. Seeing Zoe so distraught was too much for her.

Zoe turned to Spencer. "Then you're his only family I have left?" She rushed into Spencer's arms and he hugged her as tightly as he could, resting his head on her tiny shoulders as sobs began to rock her body.

"Shh, it'll be okay, Zoe," Spencer whispered, stroking her hair. "I'm here."

He glanced at Raina, and her eyes were glistening with tears.

"I'm so happy I have you, Spence," Zoe said against his cheek.

"And you always will." He kissed her cheek. "I'll always be here for you. I promise."

Zoe looked up at him. "Promise? You won't leave me? Like my mommy and daddy?"

"Promise."

"Then you'll go with me to the father-daughter dance at school?" Zoe asked, wiping her tears away with the back of her hand. "It's next month before the Christmas holiday."

Spencer looked down at his niece. "I would be honored."

Zoe attempted a smile. She turned to Raina. "Can I stay home today with you and Uncle Spence?"

Raina pondered Zoe's request and Spencer could see the wheels of her mind turning. He hoped she would allow it. They had just unloaded some heavy emotional baggage on a six-year-old. She'd lost both her parents and found two of the people she cared about most had spent the night together. How could she turn down her request?

"You can." Raina nodded. "We could do something fun."

And that's exactly what they did after Spencer called the office to tell Mona he wasn't coming in and Raina feigned illness to Summer, though he doubted she believed it for a second.

To cheer Zoe up they took her to an amusement park that had breathtaking landscaping and a special VIP safari tour with hands-on activities with the wildlife for visitors. Zoe got to have two parrots sit on her shoulder while they serenaded her, feed red kangaroos from Australia, ride a one-year-old Aldabra tortoise from the Seychelles Islands and play one-on-one with the capuchin monkeys from South America. Spencer was more adventurous, holding a baby tiger in his arms while Raina took photos from afar.

Spencer couldn't remember the last time, he'd had this much fun. After he'd dropped them off after dinner, he finally made his way home. As he drove over to Star Island, Spencer examined his feelings for Raina and Zoe. He was proud that Zoe wasn't angry with him for not telling her sooner that he was her uncle. Instead she'd embraced him with open arms and asked him to her father-daughter dance. He would be able to do right by Cameron by looking after Zoe and ensuring she had all the love her heart and tiny hands could hold.

And then there was Raina. In a short time, she'd become a huge part of his life and he wouldn't have it any other way. Every time he was with her, whether they were talking, trick-or-treating, playing with the animals at the amusement park or making love until the wee hours of the morning, he fell harder for her. There was no doubt in his mind he'd fallen in love with Raina Martin, and he couldn't wait to see what was in store next.

Raina showed up to the catering shop with coffee and a variety of muffins and scones in hand. She knew she was in the doghouse for leaving Summer in the lurch the day before they had a large dinner party to prepare for.

When she arrived the lights were already on, but the front of the shop was empty. Raina heard pots and pans clanging from the back of the house. She reached for a nearby white linen napkin and cracked the swinging door open. She waved the napkin back and forth like a white flag.

"May I come in?" she asked from the other side of the door.

"You'd better," Summer yelled. "'Cause we have a lot of work to do."

Raina steeled herself for the choice words she was sure Summer had for her and walked inside the kitchen with her box of muffins and coffee outstretched.

Summer eyed her peace offering warily and then

said, "Just put mine on the counter." She returned to the root vegetables she was preparing at her station.

"Listen, Summer," Raina began., "I'm really sorry about yesterday."

"Raina, I understand you've found love and all that," Summer replied. "But we still have a business to run. And you and I—" she pointed to Raina "—are it. I can't be down staff. Thankfully, my sister came in and was able to pitch in yesterday when you bailed."

Raina swallowed hard. She knew Summer was right, but that wasn't the only reason she hadn't come in. "I know you're mad at me," she said finally. "And you have every reason to be. Can I just tell you why I didn't come in?"

Summer rolled her eyes. "Do I have a choice?"

Raina smiled. She and Summer had been friends a long time and she knew this too would pass. She just had to get over the hard part. She walked over and placed Summer's favorite drink and a large blueberry scone in front of her.

Summer stopped what she was doing long enough to reach for the drink and bring it to her lips. She turned to face Raina and waited for the explanation.

"Again, you're right that I shouldn't have left you hanging yesterday," Raina replied. "But Zoe caught Spencer at my place."

"After he'd spent the night?"

Raina nodded. "She was rather excited and was talking about us becoming a family."

"Is that what you want?" Summer inquired.

Raina didn't answer because she wasn't ready to think about exactly what her relationship with Spencer might lead to. She said instead, "So we finally told her that Spencer was her uncle."

"You did? How'd she take that?"

"Oh, she was thrilled at first," Raina responded. "But then she started asking about her father and where he was." She watched as understanding began to dawn on Summer. "And you guessed it, we had to tell her that not only had she lost her mother, but her father was dead, too."

Summer touched her chest in concern. "Oh, Lord, that poor child. She must have been devastated."

"She was distraught and there was no way I was going to send her to school in that condition," Raina said. "So I allowed her to stay home from school and Spencer and I took her to the amusement park to cheer her up."

"Well that was a very *family* thing to do."

Summer's comment was not lost on Raina. She was trying to press her on defining exactly what was going on between them. "Spencer was really great with Zoe. He seemed to know exactly what to say to comfort her. Zoe was putty in his hands."

"Zoe's not the only one," Summer said underneath her breath.

"All right, Summer," Raina said. "Say what you have to say."

"I'm already saying it. I *want* you to see where it goes with Spencer. It could be good for you. I just think you're going too fast and now you're talking family. You've barely known him a few weeks. I mean, do you two even know what you're doing?" Summer asked.

"I don't understand."

"I'm just playing devil's advocate here, but you and

Spencer have both lost siblings close to you in dramatic ways. Could you be clinging to each other as a lifeline because it's an easy way out?"

Raina frowned. She'd never thought of her relationship with Spencer as a cop-out or a crutch. "Absolutely not! How could you think that?"

Summer groaned heavily. "Okay, okay. I had to ask." She walked over to Raina and grabbed her by the shoulders. "Listen, I'm just concerned for you. I know it's been a while since you've had a serious relationship, and Spencer comes along at the right time after you've lost Alexa. And Zoe needs a father and it's all so neat and convenient that I question if you're thinking clearly. Perhaps you're still grieving? What happens in a few months?"

Raina pulled away. "Well, I'd hope we're still seeing each other." She couldn't bear it if she and Spencer ended just as quickly as they'd begun. Summer was right. They had gotten close in a short time. If she admitted the truth to herself, she was in love with Spencer Davis. She didn't know how he felt about her because neither of them had said anything directly, but the way he treated her, made love to her, told her there were genuine feelings behind their relationship. He'd told her he'd fallen for her. Could she hope that he'd meant love?

"I hope for your sake that's true, Raina, and that he doesn't fall back into his old patterns," Summer said.

"So do I. So do I."

Chapter 13

November flew by. When she wasn't catering, taking Zoe to one of her numerous weekend outings or to her grandparents', Raina spent as much time as possible with Spencer. She'd missed him terribly when he'd gone away for nearly a week to court several new clients in New York and Philadelphia. When he'd returned, Spencer had more than made up for it by giving her a beautiful diamond teardrop necklace and making sweet love to her for hours. Having been away from her for days, he'd been insatiable and they'd made love in the bedroom, in the shower, in the infinity pool and outside his Star Island home underneath the stars on one of the chaises facing the bay.

Raina blushed at the memory as she stirred butter into the mashed potatoes she was making at her parent's home for Thanksgiving dinner. She and Zoe had come several hours earlier so she could help her mother with the meal. Of course, her mother hated having Raina in the kitchen because she wanted to make everything even though Raina was a well-known chef.

But she'd finally conceded, allowing Raina to make the easiest dish, mashed potatoes, and a dessert. Raina decided to add something a little extra to give the potatoes some zest. And for dessert, she'd prepared a sweet potato and white chocolate bread pudding that was sure to be a crowd-pleaser.

Spencer was due any minute, as was Summer, her boyfriend and her parents, who were close friends with Raina's parents. Raina hoped that having company would help alleviate any tension between her parents and Spencer. Although they knew Spencer was a part of her life and they were dating, her parents were not pleased and didn't attempt to hide their displeasure at her choice of companion.

The doorbell rang and the guests began arriving. Her mother went to greet them. Summer's parents were first, followed by Spencer. On his heels were Summer and Ryan. Summer had brought a brown butter cake and buttermilk mascarpone ice cream that she'd had on dry ice. The Newmans stayed in the living room with her parents while Spencer, Summer and Ryan joined her in the kitchen.

"Happy Thanksgiving," Summer said. She gave Raina a quick hug. Ryan was right behind her and kissed her cheek.

"Happy Thanksgiving." Raina looked up to see Spencer in the doorway. He was smiling at her and holding an expensive bottle of wine. He was wearing dark trousers and a dress shirt opened at the nape with a blazer over it. "Put the ice cream here." She opened the freezer for Summer.

"That cake looks delicious, Summer," Spencer commented, taking in her concoction on the counter.

"Thank you." Summer smiled proudly. She was beginning to get used to Spencer's presence in Raina's life despite her misgivings about how quickly they'd started dating. Sometimes he would come and steal Raina away from the shop for lunch.

Spencer filled the kitchen with his strong masculine presence. He leaned down to brush his lips across Raina's. "Hey, beautiful." He eyed the teardrop necklace he'd given her, which was displayed on her neck. She was wearing a V-neck sweater dress with a chunky belt that hit just above the knee and stiletto boots.

"Hey, yourself." Raina radiated a smile up at the man she'd come to love. Her heart turned over at how handsome and sexy he was.

"Where's my munchkin?" he asked.

"She's with her grandfather in the study watching football."

"I think I'll go join them."

"I'll join you," Ryan said at his heel. "I'm sure the two ladies want to have some girl talk." The two men left the room.

"He seems to be making himself comfortable," Summer commented, taking a seat at the kitchen table.

"Yeah, but my parents aren't making it easy for him." Raina joined her. "They still see him as a threat."

"Well, we both know how they felt about Alexa."

"What are you talking about?"

"C'mon, Raina, this is me you're talking to. I grew

up right next to you. Do you think I didn't see how your parents favored Alexa over you? It was so obvious."

"Really?" And Raina had always thought no one had seen the truth. She'd always kept the hurt she'd felt about their indifference to herself as if it were a cross she had to bear. Why had she never confided in Summer? Perhaps because she was ashamed, embarrassed?

Summer leaned back toward the hallway to make sure no one was coming. "Yes, really." She touched Raina's arm. "But you never said anything to me, never complained. It's why I liked you so much. You were so strong and stalwart. You could just never see that."

Raina dropped her lashes quickly to hide the hurt. "Thank you for saying that. It means a lot."

"I didn't say it to be nice. I said it because I meant it." Both women reached for each other almost simultaneously and hugged.

"I'm so lucky to have a friend like you, Summer."

"What's going on here?" Spencer had returned and was holding Zoe in his arms. "Or can anyone get in on the action?

Somehow Zoe's outfit had changed from the jumper Raina had had her wear to a dress her mother had selected. Raina rolled her eyes upward for strength. *It's going to be a long night.*

Hours later, after their bellies were full, everyone sat around eating the delicious desserts Raina and Summer had prepared. Although Summer's brown butter cake was delicious; it was Raina's sweet potato and white chocolate bread pudding with hot caramel sauce that Spencer loved. Like everything she made, the bread pudding was perfect, not too mushy, but firm and slightly crispy on the outside.

Earlier, when they'd said what they were thankful for, Spencer had made no secret of how thankful he was that he'd met Raina and discovered he had a niece. Unfortunately, that was when the peaceful evening starting going downhill.

He'd just returned from taking the dessert dishes from the dining room to the kitchen, where Raina and Summer were washing dishes, when he heard Crystal tell Summer's mother what a chore it was to put up with Spencer, an intruder into her family. Thankfully, Zoe, her grandfather, Ryan and Mr. Newman had returned to the study to watch football and they couldn't hear the women talking.

Spencer's blood began to boil. He'd had it up to here with Crystal's disrespect. For over a month, he'd put up with her dismissive attitude or her completely ignoring his presence as if he didn't exist. Well, he wasn't going anywhere and it was high time she knew it.

He stepped into the dining room and the two women broke apart from their huddle.

"Spencer, must you sneak up on folks?" Crystal asked haughtily.

"I'm six foot four and wear a size fourteen shoe, Mrs. Martin," Spencer returned. "It's pretty hard for me to sneak up on anybody."

She scowled at him, while Mrs. Newman looked properly embarrassed at having been caught discussing him.

"What is it that you have against me, Mrs. Martin?" Spencer inquired. "I have done nothing but treat you and your husband with respect, love your granddaughter, my niece—"

"Don't you dare talk about my granddaughter," Crystal interrupted. "You know nothing about her. You've been around for, what, a couple of months?" She snapped her finger and the vitriol she must have been carrying for months came spewing out. "And you think that entitles you to a place in her life, a life your brother couldn't bother to be a part of?"

Spencer tried to calm himself, but he was having a hard time given that she had no idea what she was talking about. His voice rose when he spoke, booming through the house. "Ah, so you're finally being honest. You don't want me to have a part or say in Zoe's life. Well I'm sorry to tell you, Mrs. Martin, but you're not the only one who cares about her. I have rights, too.…"

Raina must have heard the rising voices, because she and Summer came rushing into the dining room, "What's going on?" she asked. She looked at Spencer first and then dead center at her mother. "Mother?"

Crystal came forward and reached for her hand. "Spencer here was just telling us how he has rights, too. Isn't that what he said?" She looked to Mrs. Newman for backup, but she remained silent.

Raina sighed. "Mom, it's Thanksgiving. Can't we all just get along?"

"No," her mother said, her voice getting more shaky. "I don't trust him." She pointed to Spencer. "He's just waiting for an opportunity to take Zoe away from us."

"That's ridiculous. Tell her she's wrong," Raina said, glancing at Spencer and then back her mother. "That's she's completely off base."

"She is," he responded. "All I want is to be a part and to have a say in Zoe's life."

Raina turned around to face him with a bewildered look. "A say?"

"Can we talk about this privately?" He wanted some time alone with Raina so calmer heads could prevail.

"No," Raina stated emphatically. "We'll talk about it now. What did you mean by a say in Zoe's life?"

"I'm Cameron's only living relative, and I'm kind of standing in for him on what he would do if he were alive. All I'm saying is that I would like to be consulted on Zoe's care, her education...." His voice drifted off.

"As if we were sharing custody?" Raina asked. "Why have you never mentioned this before?"

"I don't know," Spencer said, even though he knew why he hadn't said anything. He'd just assumed that given where his and Raina's relationship was headed that it would be a moot point. "I thought we were on the same page on the role I would have in Zoe's life."

"Role?" Raina laughed bitterly as if the idea was ludicrous. "Where were you in the middle of the night when Alexa was giving birth to Zoe? Were you in the delivery room getting your hand squeezed to death as Zoe was brought into this world?" As Raina threw more questions at him her voice steadily grew louder and louder. She wasn't upset about him visiting but that he wanted to be consulted on decisions concerning Zoe. "Where were you when Zoe came down with the chicken pox and we had to rub calamine lotion all over her body? Where were you when Zoe woke up screaming in the middle of the night when she realized her mommy was gone? Nowhere!"

"Exactly!" her mother chimed in. He could see that

Crystal was glad she'd caused discord between him and Raina.

"And whose fault was that, Raina?" Spencer inquired softly, trying to calm the situation. "Certainly not mine, nor my brother's. In case you have short-term memory loss, Alexa never told us."

"And why is that?" Raina asked. "Because your brother was a drunk and a dope addict."

She'd touched a spark, and Spencer roared, "Don't you dare talk about my brother! You don't know the first thing about him."

"I didn't have to know him—he was in the papers. Why else would my sister keep the truth from him? She obviously thought he was a bad influence and wanted to keep him away from Zoe."

Zoe, the object of all the yelling, came running into the room. "Why are you yelling at each other? It's Thanksgiving!" She looked at Spencer and then at Raina and her grandmother, who were both starting to cry.

Spencer reached Zoe first and picked her up. "I'm sorry, sweetie," he said. He could see Raina and her mother were far from happy that he was holding her. "We all just had a disagreement. We're sorry if our voices got a little loud."

A smile formed on Zoe's mouth. "It's all right, Uncle Spence." She gave him a kiss on the cheek. "Just keep it down, okay? I'm trying to watch the game."

"Sure thing, munchkin." Spencer placed her back on her feet and seconds later she was scurrying out of the room and back to the study.

Spencer glanced around the room at the sour expressions on the Martin women's faces and said, "I think it's best if I leave."

"I think that would be best," Crystal retorted smugly.

But Spencer couldn't care less what she said or what she thought about him; he looked at Raina. "Can we talk later? I'll be at my penthouse."

Raina didn't speak. She merely nodded.

Dejected, Spencer left the room, grabbed his coat from the coatrack in the foyer and departed. He felt terrible for nearly ruining Zoe's first Thanksgiving without her mother, but Crystal and Raina had finally rubbed his nerves raw and he'd exploded. Worse was the betrayed look he'd seen in Raina's eyes. She looked as if she'd been mortally wounded.

He'd thought when he hadn't pursued custody legally that she'd come to realize that his presence in Zoe's life was important. Perhaps he had been living with blinders on, content with the status quo? He had never told her that he wanted to be consulted on Zoe's care because he'd known for a while now that Raina was the woman he was going to marry. And if they got married, custody and Zoe's care wouldn't be an issue between them.

And now he'd mucked it all up. He loved Raina. Her beauty, her smarts, her fire, all qualities that he loved. He couldn't bear to think he'd done something to jeopardize that.

When he finally got to the penthouse, he made a beeline for the refrigerator and popped open a bottle of beer. He was surprised when his doorbell rang, but he was hopeful Raina would be standing on the other side, ready to talk. And not just about Zoe, but about the two of them.

He walked over and eagerly swung open the door to find Ty on the other side. He couldn't hide his disappointment and concern was on his best friend's face.

"Well, you're finally home," Ty said, sauntering into the penthouse.

"What do you mean?" Spencer asked, following him into the kitchen.

"Well you've been pretty MIA of late," Ty said, heading for the fridge and reaching for a beer. He popped it open and took a swig. "And after leaving my parents for dinner, I took a chance you'd be home."

"Have I been MIA?" Spencer asked, scratching his head.

"Uh, yeah," Ty responded. "I've called you a few times and you haven't returned my calls. Are you that sprung?"

Spencer chuckled. "Okay. Maybe I have been a little preoccupied, but you know how it is."

"I do. It's how it was when I met Brielle." Ty took another sip of beer. "But you, I've never seen you this… this engrossed in a woman before."

"Well, Raina is an amazing woman. And Zoe." Spencer shrugged. "What can I say? My niece is an awesome kid. Alexa did a great job raising her."

"Now you're getting me worried," Ty said. "You didn't listen to a word I said, did you? You've gotten attached much too soon."

"I disagree," Spencer said. "Zoe is my niece, Cameron's child. She needs a father. I mean, an uncle."

"And you're ready to be a father? Because the more time you spend with your niece, the more she's going to regard you as a substitute."

"And what's so wrong that?" Spencer didn't understand why Ty was being so negative and not being supportive. Spencer had had his doubts when Ty had gotten involved with Brielle, a former exotic dancer, but he'd been supportive of their union. And they'd been married for four years now.

Ty's voice rose. "What's wrong is your emotions are still running high because you've never gotten over losing Cameron. And after the dust has settled and some time has passed, I fear you'll see things differently. And where will that put Raina and your niece, who've become accustomed to having you in their life?"

"This isn't some flash in the pan," Spencer said tersely. "I have feelings for Raina. *Real feelings.* They are not imaginary feelings that I've cooked up to cope with losing my brother."

"Have you told her that Alexa came to you looking for Cameron and that you sent her away? Did you tell her Zoe could have had a father had you not interfered?"

The question threw Spencer. It reminded him of what he'd tried hard to forget, which was that Alexa could have been trying to contact Cameron to tell him he was going to be a father when he'd refused to give her Cameron's number. Spencer didn't have a chance to answer because Raina was standing in the doorway to his kitchen, looking shell-shocked.

He'd given her a key a couple of weeks ago after a late meeting had forced her to wait downstairs with the doormen until he'd arrived. He could never have imagined that she would use it at the one moment he needed privacy.

"What?" she asked, perplexed.

Ty spun around and saw that Raina was standing behind him. Spencer meanwhile couldn't move. He was frozen in place and terrified that the world he'd created over the past couple of months would crumble.

When he didn't speak, Raina asked, "My sister came

to you? She came looking for Cameron to tell him about Zoe?"

"We don't know that for sure," Ty replied. "I was just speculating."

Raina glared at him for trying to protect his best friend. "And why would you think that, Ty?"

Ty looked at Spencer, unsure of how to answer. Spencer wasn't sure he knew, either, but he finally spoke. "The timing."

Raina looked at him and waited for him to continue.

Ty spoke up instead. "I'm going to get out of here and back home to Brielle. I think the two of you need to be alone."

"That would be a good idea," Spencer said sternly. He wanted to recount the story in private to Raina.

Ty nodded and left the room. Seconds later, Spencer heard the click of the front door closing.

"Well?" Raina said, folding her arms across her chest.

Spencer paused for several beats. "Once news of another of Cameron's affairs hit the papers several weeks into his affair with Alexa, Cameron broke it off with Alexa. She wasn't pleased about it. She kept calling him until he eventually changed his number."

"Is that when she came to you?"

Spencer nodded. "She asked to meet me and I felt bad. I knew she was hurting over the breakup, so I did. She begged me for his new phone number. I knew my brother could be a real jerk and I didn't want her to get hurt more than she already was. I advised her to move on, that he wasn't coming back."

"And when did you meet her?"

He sighed. He knew where she was going with the

question and he answered honestly. It was all he could do if he wanted her to trust him. "A couple of months later."

"So she could very well have been trying to find him to tell him that he was going to be a father and that she was pregnant with Zoe?"

Spencer stared Raina dead in the eye and said, "Yes. I don't know for sure, but it's a strong possibility."

"So Zoe could have had a father if it hadn't been for your interference?"

"Listen, Raina." Spencer began walking toward her, but she stepped back away from him.

"I don't want to hear it, Spencer. My sister came to you for help and you turned her away. And now here you are years later trying to assuage your own guilt for what could have been avoided."

"That's not fair, Raina," Spencer said. "You can't blame me for this. Alexa could have spoken up. If she'd told me she was pregnant, I would have moved heaven and earth to help her, to get Cameron to see reason and step up to the plate."

"Like you did to help him get clean?"

Spencer stared at her in disbelief. How could she say such a horrible thing to him? She knew how hard it was for him to forgive himself for not being able to help his brother get sober. Why was it that the one person you loved the most could hurt you so deeply?

"Now I understand why Alexa's dying words were to go to you. That you'd help me. She knew Cameron had passed away a couple of years before because his death had been splashed across the Miami papers. She knew you would be *compelled* to help me."

When he remained silent, Raina kept going. "Nothing to say? I'm surprised. You've been pounding your chest about your rights and what my family and I have been denying you when all along you could have been Zoe's uncle if you had lifted a finger to help my sister."

"It's so easy for you to put the blame on me and make me the scapegoat, isn't it, Raina?" Spencer responded coldly. "Instead of looking to Alexa. She was the wrong party here. *She* was the one who had an affair with a married man and got pregnant. *She* was the one who set all of this in motion by not being honest."

"No, no, no." Raina covered her ears. "How can you put the blame on my dead sister? You're being cruel."

"Because it's the truth! So what, I didn't give her Cameron's phone number? She could have easily hired a lawyer, found Cameron and served him with paternity papers just like you did to me. But she didn't. She wanted to be a martyr and act like the big bad athlete had done her a disservice. Perhaps you should look a little closer to home for who you're truly angry at and not at me."

Clearly, Raina didn't like what he said, because she replied, "I don't have to listen to this. You've been sitting on this info for months, worming your way into my life, into Zoe's, to appease your own guilt." She turned on her heel and left the kitchen, but Spencer was not going to give her the last word.

With three long strides, he caught up with her in the living room. "Yes, I didn't tell you why I suspected Alexa came to me, but I haven't been worming my way into your life because I feel guilty. Initially it may have started like that, but I don't feel guilty anymore."

"Oh yeah? Why is that?" Raina asked.

"Because I've grown to care for you, Raina," he said

softly. With his free hand, he caressed her hair and then her cheek. "The past couple of months with you and Zoe have been the best of my life."

"Don't, Spencer…" Raina tugged her arm to pull away from him, but his grip was tight.

He could feel her resistance to his words, but he was determined to get through to her. He had to. He didn't want to lose her. He released her arm and cupped her cheek and forced her to look up at him. "I've fallen for you, Raina Martin. I'm in love with you."

"You're what?" She looked up at him with such surprise that Spencer couldn't resist lowering his head to have a taste of her lips. It was a light and soft kiss at first, but then it grew more urgent, more passionate, and his tongue began to play at the sides of her mouth until she parted her lips. He wasted no time, darting his tongue inside to touch hers. He pulled her firmly to him, cupping her buttocks, and she moaned against him as he delved deeper and deeper into the recesses of her mouth.

She tasted so good that he could go on forever. He would have if she hadn't begun resisting him. "Spencer, stop. Stop."

Her words finally cut through the fog and his passion to register and he released her. "What's wrong?"

"What's wrong is that a lot has been said tonight. And I'm confused."

"Are you confused about your feelings for me?" Spencer inquired. "Tell me you don't feel the same way about me. Because if you do, I'll know you're lying." She couldn't kiss him like that if she felt nothing for him.

"I need time to process all of this," Raina responded,

flailing her arms about. "Between my parents, Zoe, you, Alexa and Cameron, I'm so confused. I need to go, and you need to let me."

"If I let you go, will you come back to me?" Spencer asked. Despite everything that had happened at her parents' home, she'd still come to him tonight to talk, so he knew they'd made progress. A couple of months ago, Raina would have never come to him to hear his side of the story. He'd slowly chipped away at the walls she'd erected around her to let him in. He didn't want to go backward and have her shut him out again. He loved her with all his heart. He couldn't lose her.

"I guess you're just going to have to wait and see," Raina said quietly before walking out of his penthouse.

Chapter 14

Raina was thoroughly confused by the turn of events. So much had happened in the course of the night that she didn't know what to do. She drove home on autopilot. She'd left Zoe at her parents because she hadn't known how long her conversation with Spencer would take.

Raina was thankful for the solace so she could allow her mind to wander and not worry about what her six-year-old niece was doing or how she was coping on her first Thanksgiving without Alexa. And wander her mind did. Spencer wanted a say in how Zoe was raised? Alex came to Spencer and he didn't tell her? Spencer was in love with her? Any one of these questions was enough to send her mind whirling, but all three?

As she entered her house from the garage, Raina automatically punched in the security password and set the alarm. Then she went upstairs to her master bedroom and sat on the damask-covered bed. She fumbled with the zipper of her knee-high stiletto boots before the catch finally released and she eased them one after the other down her toned legs. When she was done, she unbuckled the belt over her sweater dress and reached over her head to remove the dress and her undies. Padding into the restroom, she turned on the taps of her jetted bathtub and poured a generous amount of bubble bath in.

While she waited for the tub to fill up, she went downstairs in the nude to uncork a bottle of wine and pour herself a glass before returning upstairs to sink into the luxurious lavender-scented water. Lying back in the tub with her glass of wine, she thought about the day. *How could it all have gone so terribly wrong and right at the same time?*

Although Spencer had never said anything, in her heart of hearts, she'd always known that he wanted a larger role. He loved his niece and felt responsible for her. But her mother just had to keep poking the tiger until Spencer had snapped. Despite his anger at her mother, Raina didn't believe Spencer would take her to court to force the issue because it wouldn't be in Zoe's best interest. But she had to be willing to compromise.

Raina took a large sip of her pinot noir.

What she wasn't so sure about was whether she could forgive his lie of omission. Alexa had come to him years ago, pregnant and alone and needing help, and Spencer had covered for his brother and sent her away. Perhaps if Cameron had known about Zoe, knew he was going to be a father, he would have cleaned up his act. Perhaps he'd still be with them today.

But was Spencer the only one to blame? He had a point. Alexa could have spoken up. She could have come clean and told Spencer about her condition. Better yet, she could have told Cameron about Zoe years before his death in a car crash. Zoe had been two years old when he'd died. Was it fair to solely blame Spencer for her twin's shortcomings?

Alexa was not blameless by any means, Raina thought as she indulged in more wine. She'd knowingly had an affair with a married man. Their parents had taught them the difference between right and wrong. But then again, they had always held Alexa to a different standard. She'd been so high on her pedestal, she probably thought she was justified in whatever she did, including sleeping with a married man.

But Spencer should have told her the truth from the start; he shouldn't have kept the fact that Alexa had come to him seven years ago from her. It did make her doubtful if she could believe the last thing he'd said to her. That he'd fallen in love with her. *Did he really mean it?*

She sure hoped he meant it because then it would mean she wasn't alone in her feelings. She'd been in love with Spencer for a while, but she hadn't dared to say the words aloud for fear he didn't feel the same way. But he'd said it tonight. Should she take a chance and tell him that she'd fallen for him, too?

Raina lowered her empty wineglass to the ledge of the bathtub. She wasn't going to find all the answers tonight to all the questions that plagued her. After lathering her skin and rinsing off, Raina exited the bathtub and hugged a large fluffy cotton towel around her bosom. After she'd dried off and changed into a sleep shirt, she drifted off to sleep.

Spencer stared at the calendar perched on his office desk. It reminded him that the father-daughter dance with Zoe was approaching on Friday. The problem was he hadn't heard from Raina in nearly a week since she'd come to his penthouse after that disastrous Thanksgiving meal. He'd hoped after he'd revealed that he was in love with her that Raina would have come to him and repeated the words back, said she loved him as much as he loved her, but she hadn't. She'd stayed away. And it scared him. Had he lost her for good?

"Mr. Davis, Ty is on the line for you," Mona said through the intercom.

"Thank you, Mona," Spencer said and picked up the receiver to talk to his best friend.

Like Raina, Ty had been MIA for nearly a week. He probably felt bad that he'd opened his big mouth and told Raina about Spencer's involvement in Alexa's paternity reveal. But Spencer didn't blame him. He hadn't known that Raina would use her key to come to his place and overhear their conversation. Further, the truth would have come out eventually and it might as well have come out now before Spencer fell further in love with Raina only to have her walk away from him.

"Hey, man," Spencer said. "How are you?"

"The more important question," Ty said on the opposite end of the phone, "is how are you? I know I messed up royally on Thanksgiving, and I'm truly sorry."

"Listen, Ty, don't worry about it. You didn't say anything that shouldn't have been said."

Ty paused for several beats. "How's Raina?"

"Dunno. Haven't heard from her."

"It's been a week."

"I know."

"Did you guys talk at all after I left?" Ty inquired. "Doesn't she know that you're not to blame? Alexa could have told Cameron, too."

"I said as much to Raina."

"And?"

Spencer shrugged. "And nothing. She listened to what I had to say. Listened as I told her I loved her and then she left."

"Loved her?" Ty repeated Spencer's words. "Did you say *love?*"

"Yes, I did. I love Raina. I love everything about her. Her beauty, her wit, her charm, her incredible body, the incredible food she makes, her maternal instinct even though she doesn't think she has one. I love it all."

"Did you say that to her?" Ty asked. "Because if you did, I can't imagine she would have walked away."

"No, I started to say more but she was staring back at me so shocked that I was afraid to spill my guts and have her walk away. It would have devastated me, like when I lost Cam, and I doubted I would recover."

"Ouch. So what now?"

"I don't know. I guess I wait. She told me she needed time to process it and I want to give that to her, but Zoe asked me to the father-daughter dance at her school and it's coming up in a few days. What should I do?"

"You keep your word to your niece," Ty replied as if the answer was clear. "And then you tell that woman just how much you love her. And I promise you if you tell her everything you've told me, she can't help but tell you she feels the same."

"You really think so?" Spencer asked incredulously.

"I know so. Trust me on this," Ty said.

"Time will tell," Spencer responded. "Time will tell."

"What about this dress for Zoe?" Raina's mother held up a black-and-red dress with long puffy sleeves; a high waist with a bow and a pleated tulle-lined skirt.

Raina, her mother and Zoe were shopping for a dress for Zoe to go to the father-daughter dance on Friday. Although Raina hadn't spoken to Spencer after their talk over a week ago, she knew that he would come and take Zoe to the dance. Of course, her father was hoping the exact opposite because he'd said as much a few days ago when she'd indicated she hadn't spoken to Spencer. She was sure her parents would like nothing better than for Spencer to fall off the face of the earth, but Raina *knew* that would never happen.

Zoe shook her head. "Grandma, that dress is ugly."

"It's a perfect holiday dress," Crystal retorted and held up another monstrosity of a dress. It was blue and silver with a faux velvet top, flower detail at the front and ruched short sleeves with a silver sash.

"I agree with Zoe," Raina said. "It's not the right dress for her." Then she laid eyes on a beautiful red dress with lots of sparkly detail and a gorgeous long overlay skirt. She reached for it instantly and slid it off the rack and held it up to show Zoe. "This is the one."

The red dress was sleeveless with a sequin soutache detail on the bodice and a simple empire waist with a bow.

"I love it, Auntie Raina," Zoe gushed, taking the dress out of her hand. She walked over to the floor-length mirror and pranced around with it from side to side so she could see it from every angle.

"I think that dress is inappropriate," her mother said. "And it's sleeveless. In case you hadn't noticed, Raina, it's the dead of winter."

"Mom, Zoe loves the dress, look at her." They watched her in the mirror. "And she'll have her coat on over it. She'll be fine."

"Why must you always be so obstinate where Zoe's concerned? I did rear two girls."

Raina was furious with her mother's tone and grabbed her by the arm, pulling her off to the side so she could speak with her privately while still keeping an eye on Zoe. "And I'm *rearing* Zoe," Raina said. "And I'm telling you that you need to start trusting my judgment."

"You mean the judgment that had you dating the man that wants to take Zoe away from all of us? You mean that judgment?"

"Listen, Mother." Raina pointed her finger at her mother. "I've had about enough of this. I'm not going to listen to you bad-mouth Spencer. He's not to blame for Alexa's mistakes. He's right. She should have told Cameron the truth long ago. She had time. Zoe is six, nearly seven. She could have told him the truth before he died in that car crash. But *she* chose not to."

Her mother seemed genuinely offended and tears welled in her eyes at her daughter's harsh criticism. "How can you say such things about your sister? When she's dead and can't defend herself?"

"Because it's the truth, Mother, and it's time you finally start facing it." Raina sighed. "Alexa was no angel. Zoe is the result of extramarital affair."

"No, no, no." Her mother shook her head as if she

didn't want to hear Raina's words, but Raina was going to end this once and for all.

"Your precious Alexa had an affair with a married man and she chose to keep the truth from him that he'd sired a child. It was her choice to raise Zoe alone and only in her last breath did she finally give a clue about Zoe's true parentage."

Her mother broke down and started sobbing as she finally let the truth about Alexa sink in. Raina rubbed her mother's back as if she were an inconsolable child. "I'm sorry, Mama, but Alexa is gone and you've just got me. I know I may not be the first choice of daughter you would have picked to survive, but I'm here and I'm doing the best *I* can to raise Zoe."

Suddenly her mother looked up through her tears. "Why—why would you say something like…like that? I would never want anything to happen to you, Raina. Never."

"Really? You could have fooled me," Raina huffed.

"I love you, Raina," her mother said, pulling a tissue from her purse and blowing her nose. "I always have. If I paid more attention to Alexa it was because she always seemed to need it more. She had no self-confidence and never felt lovable. I think it's why she may have gone looking for it the wrong places, like with that Cameron fellow. But you? Even when you were a little girl, you were always strong and independent. If you would fall, you would just brush yourself off and get back up. But not Alexa, she would fall and cry until someone went to pick her up. Alexa *always needed* someone."

Raina nodded and tears began to descend down her cheeks. "I understand that, Mama. I do. But the thing is, I needed you, too. Sometimes I needed to be held, too."

"Oh, Raina." Her mother pulled her into her arms. "I love you, child. I always have and I always will." She stroked Raina's back as she began to cry again.

"Grandma?" Zoe came toward them after she'd finished admiring herself in the mirror. "Is everything okay?" She looked back and forth between her aunt and grandmother, who had tearstained cheeks and red eyes.

"Of course, sweetheart," her grandmother said. "Come give Grandma a hug." And together the Martin women formed one giant hug.

Spencer tugged on the tie of his suit to make sure it was straight as he stood at the doorway to Raina's home. He'd finally broken down and called her yesterday to check and see if he could still take Zoe to the father-daughter dance. Raina had said of course, as if it should be obvious to him. It hadn't been. How was he to know she hadn't changed her mind and wanted no part of him? She sure as hell had maintained silence when it had come to their relationship.

As he rang the doorbell, he was bothered by that the most, that she could disregard his feelings for her without saying anything back to him. Perhaps she didn't feel the same way and he was standing out on the ledge alone?

Raina answered the door. Despite how hurt he was, a smile instantly came to Spencer's face. She looked as beautiful as ever. She was dressed simply in black jeans and a long-sleeved black-and-white tunic, but she could have been wearing a sack and she still would have looked as sexy as hell to him.

"Come in," she said and led him to the living room to wait.

They stood awkwardly, staring at each other. Spencer wasn't sure of what to say.

Raina wrung her hands. "Um…Zoe is just about ready," she finally said, lowering her head. "I should go check on her." She reached for the banister, but Spencer touched her arm.

"Raina."

"Yes," she said, turning around to face him.

What could he say that he hadn't said? Sure, he could pour his heart out some more. Tell her she was the only woman for him. But he couldn't do it. He refused to humiliate himself even further if she didn't feel the same way. "Nothing," he said and returned his hand to his side.

"I'll be right down," Raina replied and rushed up the stairs.

Spencer used the few minutes he had to compose himself. He had to get control of his feelings. As much as it pained him, he wasn't going to keep chasing after Raina. She was going to have to come to him and tell him how she felt. He just prayed that it was sooner rather than later; otherwise he was going to lose his mind.

Seconds later, Zoe glided into the living room in a red sleeveless dress with lots of sparkle. "You look like a princess," Spencer said, bending down to Zoe's height.

"Thank you." Zoe beamed. "You look very nice, too, Uncle Spence." She tugged at his necktie, which he seldom wore.

"I thought no one had noticed," Spencer said, glancing up at Raina.

She blinked nervously and licked her lips, making Spencer want to rise to his feet and take both sides of her face in his hands and kiss her until she admitted that he was more to her than a bed partner. But he didn't. Instead, he reached behind him and produced a wrist corsage for Zoe.

Zoe's eyes grew large with excitement. "For me?"

"Who else?" He removed the corsage from the plastic container and slid it onto her tiny wrist. "There, now you're perfect." He rose to his feet and glanced at his watch. The time read 6:00 p.m. "You ready to go? Doesn't the dance start at seven?"

"Sure does," Raina answered. "You should get going."

Spencer and Zoe walked to the door. When they reached it, Raina touched his arm. "Thank you for doing this, Spencer. This means a lot to Zoe."

"And to you?"

Raina nodded. "We'll talk soon. I promise."

"I'm holding you to that," Spencer said on his way out the door.

The father-daughter dance at the elementary school was quite charming. If anyone had told him five years ago during the height of his fame that he would be accompanying a six-year-old to a school dance and enjoying every minute of it, he would have told them they were lying. But he did. He enjoyed picking Zoe up and dancing with her on the hardwood floors of the gymnasium. He enjoyed drinking too-sweet punch from one of the frazzled teachers that was chaperoning the night's events with a bunch of six-year-olds.

Spencer only wished that Cameron could have been there to see what a beautiful young girl he'd created with Alexa. Zoe really was quite special. *Pretty, smart, creative, charming, a total delight, just like her aunt,* thought Spencer.

When the evening came to a close and he'd safely tucked Zoe into the backseat, Spencer was almost sad to see it end. No matter what happened with him and Raina, he hoped to share many more such nights with his niece.

Those were the thoughts that were going through Spencer's mind just as he turned onto an intersection of a major roadway and a pickup truck sped through the red light, hitting the passenger side and sending his Bentley into a tailspin. Everything faded to black.

Chapter 15

Raina's heart was in her chest as she raced through the emergency room to the front desk. She was out of breath and coatless. "Zoe Martin, Spencer Davis, they were in a car accident." She rattled off the names to the nurses' attendant. "Where are they? Are they okay? I need to see them."

When she'd gotten the call that Spencer and Zoe had been in an accident, she'd dropped everything and rushed to the hospital. On the way, she'd called her parents, who were distraught but en route.

"Ma'am," the nurse said. "Please try and calm down."

"My…my…my niece." Raina's voice cracked. "Is only six years old. And she just lost her mother, my sister, five months ago and her father is dead. Dear God!" Her hand rushed to cover her mouth and the sob that threatened to erupt.

"I'll take you to them," the nurse said immediately. She swiftly walked in front of Raina and led her to a room in the E.R. Raina peered through the glass and saw Spencer lying still on the cot. A bandage was around his head.

"Is he, is he…" Raina couldn't get the word *dead* out of her mouth.

"No, no." The nurse shook her head and touched her arm. "He survived with a pretty bad bump on the head. He was unconscious for a bit, but he's okay. Has a broken rib and some minor cuts and bruises, but otherwise he'll be fine."

"Thank God!" Raina didn't wait for permission and rushed into the room to Spencer's side. When she reached him, she grabbed his hand in hers and surveyed the damage. He had several lacerations that would add more character to his already handsome face. He didn't look too worse for wear and Raina was thankful that he'd survived. She only hoped that Zoe was the same.

She squeezed his hand and brought it to her lips. Spencer's eyes flickered open. "Hey, you," she said, giving him a halfhearted smile. "How are you feeling?"

"As if I was hit by a truck." He attempted a joke.

"I believe you were," Raina replied. "Or at least that's what the police officer said you told them before they carted you off in the ambulance."

As if suddenly remembering where he was, Spencer tried to sit up. He looked alarmed, and his eyes darted around the room, "Zoe, where is she? Is she okay?" He looked around but didn't see her.

"I don't know," Raina said softly. "They brought me to you first. And I'm hoping Zoe is just a little banged up like you are."

When Spencer didn't look her in the eye, a horrible dread began to seep through her veins. "Spencer, what's wrong? What's wrong with Zoe?"

His eyes filled with tears and Raina gave a muffled cry. "No, not my niece, not Zoe, too," Raina began backing away from him in fear.

Spencer instantly reached for her and grabbed her arm. "She's alive," he said. "Barely." He said the word underneath his breath.

"What was that?" she asked, coming closer.

He looked up into Raina's teary eyes, "It's bad, Raina. The car was hit on the passenger side. Zoe took the brunt of it."

"Oh God." Raina touched her chest. "Where is she now?"

"They took her up to ICU, and then I heard a doctor mention something about surgery, but then I passed out."

"Surgery?" Raina was horrified. "I have to find a doctor." Without another word to Spencer, she rushed out the double doors in search of a doctor. She found one and stopped him.

"I'm Zoe Martin's aunt," Raina said, touching his arm. "I'd like to know about her condition."

The doctor stared at her, perplexed for a moment, before saying, "Oh, yes, the little girl from the car accident."

"Yes, yes, that's her," Raina said. "I want to know what happened."

"We all do." Suddenly her parents materialized at Raina's side. She hadn't even seen them come in, but she was glad they were there. "What's the prognosis, Doctor?"

"Well, Zoe suffered the worst impact from the crash because the truck hit the passenger side."

"Oh, Lord!" her mother exclaimed. Raina thought she might pass out, but her father wrapped his arms around her middle and held her up.

"And?" Raina prodded him for more information.

"She suffered a concussion from the impact of the air bag, but the major injury is a ruptured spleen from crushing her pelvis," the doctor said. "Caused a lot of internal bleeding."

"What are you going to do about that?" Spencer said from behind them.

Raina was shocked to see that Spencer had moved from his bed to find out about Zoe when he had a head trauma himself. He was barefoot and wearing a hospital gown and had a bandage around his head, but he didn't seem to care.

"Sir, you need to get back in bed," the doctor said and started ushering him back toward the room he'd just left. "You suffered a serious concussion and loss of consciousness—we need you to rest."

"Not until I know about my niece," Spencer said, pulling away. "So finish telling us what you've done and what you're going to do."

Despite his injury, Spencer commanded attention with his voice and his height and the doctor acquiesced. Raina went to Spencer's side so he could lean on her as the doctor spoke.

"Well, she suffered a lot of internal bleeding from the crash. We did a physical exam that showed some abdominal tenderness, so we're doing a CT scan to see the extent of injuries."

"And what do you think it'll show?" Raina asked.

"Your niece will need surgery," the doctor replied. "Most likely to remove a portion or all of her spleen."

"Oh, God." Crystal turned to her husband and began sobbing, so Anthony quietly moved her away from the group.

"Does Zoe need her spleen?" Raina inquired.

"She doesn't need a spleen to survive, but being without your spleen increases the risk of serious infections," he answered. "But I think it's the best course of action in this situation."

"That sounds serious," Raina said. "Zoe is only six. Isn't there some other noninvasive measure you could take?"

"We could keep Zoe in the hospital to observe her condition and provide nonsurgical care, such as blood transfusion, but surgery really would be the best option."

"Raina," Spencer said, "surgery is what's best for Zoe."

"What if I disagree?" Raina replied, facing him. "Surgery is a big step."

The doctor must have figured they were Zoe's parents, because he stepped away. "Why don't you both talk about it and let me know what you'd like to do."

Once he'd gone, Raina began to speak, but Spencer pulled her into the room he'd vacated. "This is my decision," Raina began.

"No, it's not," Spencer said as he slowly made his way back to the bed. "I may not be Zoe's legal guardian, but you know as well as I do that like you, I'm the closest she has to family."

"But surgery?" Raina said and began pacing the floor. "What if something goes wrong? Oh, my God,

Spencer, I can't take that chance. I can't bear to lose her, not after losing Alexa. And my parents, they would—"

"Come here," Spencer said and Raina allowed herself to go into his comforting arms. "I know surgery is scary." He lifted her chin, so she could look up at him. "But do you really want a wait-and-see approach and Zoe could get worse and worse? If they do the surgery now, she'll be on her way to recovery."

"I guess you're right," Raina replied. "I'm—I'm just scared. She's so young."

"I know, sweetheart," Spencer said. "And it'll be okay. I promise. I promise." He kissed her forehead, then her cheek and then brushed his lips across hers.

It wasn't a kiss meant to illicit passion. It was a comforting kiss letting Raina know that Spencer wasn't going anywhere. He was there for the duration. She could count on him.

The next several hours as Raina, Spencer, her parents and even Summer and Ryan waited for Zoe to come out of surgery from her splenectomy were some of the worst Raina could remember. She'd thought she'd endured the worst of what life had to offer when she'd watched Alexa waste slowly away until she was a shell of her former self. But Zoe was young and full of promise, with so much living ahead of her. It was devastating for Raina to think her short life could be snubbed out in an instant.

Raina paced the floor of the waiting room, wishing, hoping, praying, until Summer finally whisked her off to the small chapel in the hospital to say a prayer with her. Spencer had tried to stay with her, but the doctors and nurses had been adamant that he lie down for a bit or risk injuring himself. Raina had promised to get him the moment she heard anything. It had been a struggle, but he'd relented and gone to bed.

Raina sat in the chapel first and then she kneeled at the small altar and made deals with God that if he could just spare Zoe's life, she would ensure she grew up to be an exceptional human being. Then she'd gotten angry and told God that it wasn't fair and he couldn't take away another person she loved.

"Believe, Raina," Summer said, coming to Raina's side and squeezing her shoulders. "If you believe it, it can come true."

Tears streamed down Raina's cheeks. "I'm trying, Summer, but it's not that easy. I almost lost the two people I love most in this world." She wiped her runny nose with the back of her hand.

"Two people?" Summer asked softly, squeezing Raina hands.

Raina rose to her feet and nodded. "Yes, two people. I love him, Summer. I was just too scared to admit it. And…I—I almost lost him tonight." Raina covered her mouth to smother a sob. "And if I had, he would have never known how I truly feel."

"Then you're very lucky," Summer said. "You get another chance to make things right, to tell Spencer how you truly feel about him. Not many people get that chance. And I'm sorry I gave you a hard time about Spencer. I just wanted you to be sure and I didn't want you to get hurt."

Raina nodded in agreement. "I know, but is it too much to ask God for another miracle? That he spares Zoe and that she's okay? I need to be able to tell her how much I love her and that I'm happy to be her mother."

Summer's voice was choked, but she managed to say, "No, it's not too much to ask. And I believe it's going to come true."

They bowed their heads in prayer again. Raina didn't know how long she and Summer sat together in the chapel before her mother rushed in with her father at her heels.

"Zoe's okay," her mother said, flying toward Raina and pulling her off the bench. "She made it through surgery and she's going to be okay."

"Oh, thank God!" Raina said and enveloped her mother in a hug. Summer and her father joined in and Raina's entire family shared hugs.

When they released each other, Raina asked, "Has anyone told Spencer?" She looked from her mother and then to her father.

"No, baby girl," her father said with kind eyes. "We thought you might want to tell him the good news."

Raina smiled. "Thank you. I'll do that." She squeezed her father's hand and looked him in the eye. He didn't have to say a word, but she knew that he'd finally come to terms that Spencer was a permanent fixture in their lives.

Raina started for the door, but Summer shouted out, "And you'll tell him what we discussed? Because there's no better time than the present."

"I will, I will." She couldn't wait to tell Spencer that she loved him with all her heart.

She found Spencer sleeping soundly in the private room that they'd had to browbeat him into on the fourth floor. He hadn't wanted to leave her side in the waiting room, but he'd complained of dizziness and a headache and Raina knew he had to rest. He couldn't risk making his injuries worse just to stay by her side. She was a strong woman; she would be fine. Plus, she'd had her parents and Summer by her side.

She pulled a chair closer toward Spencer's sleeping form. Then she reached across to grasp his large masculine hand in hers. His hands dwarfed her small ones, but he was a gentle giant that she'd come to love dearly.

Spencer's eyes fluttered open. She watched him try to focus on her. He assessed her eyes for some sign of sadness and when he saw none, she saw him visibly relax.

"She's okay, Spencer," Raina assured him. "And is in recovery. They'll have to monitor her over the next twenty-four hours, but she has an excellent diagnosis for a full recovery and to reclaim her spot as the most audacious little girl ever."

Spencer smiled. "I'm so glad, baby," he said drowsily. "And you? How are you?"

Raina swallowed. "I'm okay now that the both of you are safe and sound."

"Well, I'm an ox," Spencer said. "It takes a lot to take me down."

Raina laughed. "I see that." She watched him wince when he tried to move on the bed. She patted his hand. "You just get some rest. I'll be here when you wake up."

Spencer eyed her suspiciously for several moments as if he didn't believe her. "Promise?"

"I promise." Raina used her index finger to cross her heart.

"Okay," Spencer said and his eyes drifted shut again.

Raina released a deep sigh of relief. He and Zoe had pulled through the accident. She was a lucky woman, and when Spencer was coherent enough to listen, she wouldn't waste a second longer to tell him how she felt.

Raina bounced between Zoe's room in ICU to Spencer's room throughout the course of the night and early morning. Zoe was doing just fine and sleeping comfortably. She'd briefly awoken during the night and Raina had told her she'd been in an accident and had surgery. Zoe had merely nodded while Raina had just been thankful to see her beautiful brown eyes, if even for a second, before she'd drifted back to sleep. Raina left Zoe's room soon after to go back to Spencer.

She was glad she had because when she returned Spencer was shifting uncomfortably back and forth on the bed in the throes of one of his nightmares. He hadn't had one of them in well over a month since they'd been together. Had the accident caused a setback?

"No!" Spencer sat upright in the bed.

Raina rushed to his bed to join him. "Spencer, it's okay." She wrapped her arms around his middle and held him tight. "It's okay."

Spencer looked around the room in a daze before his haunted eyes finally focused on Raina. "Zoe! Dear God, Raina, we were in an accident and the car crashed into her. I'm so sorry." He began crying. "Why...why do I always survive and the people I l-love...die?"

"Oh, Spencer." She turned his head to hers so he could look into her eyes. "Zoe isn't dead. She's okay. She had to have surgery, but she'll make a full recovery."

"What?" Spencer asked, dumbfounded, wiping the sleep from his eyes with one bandaged hand.

Raina nodded. "Zoe's okay. She had to have her

spleen removed and she's pretty banged up, but she's going to be fine."

Fresh tears began flowing down Spencer's cheeks. "Are you sure?"

"Yes." Raina nodded enthusiastically. "And if you want, I can take you to see for yourself."

"I'd like that."

"Okay." She jumped off the bed and held her hand out to help Spencer. He wrapped his arms around her shoulders and they slowly made their way out of the room and into the hallway. When a nurse saw them, she insisted that Spencer sit in a wheelchair, and secured one for them so Raina could take him upstairs to the ICU.

The smile that spread across Spencer's face when he laid eyes on Zoe for himself was enough to warm Raina's heart and left no doubt that he was the man for her.

"She's beautiful, isn't she?" Spencer asked. "She looks just like Cam did when we were little."

"Really?"

"Yeah," Spencer said. "She has Cam's round face, his nose and those big brown eyes of his."

They sat looking at Zoe for a while before Raina began rolling Spencer back to his room. "Can we stop at the chapel?" Spencer asked.

"Uh, sure," Raina said and pressed the elevator to the chapel several floors below.

Once they arrived, Spencer lit a candle and said some sort of prayer Raina couldn't hear. She gave him his quiet time and sat on the bench behind him.

When he finally turned around, his eyes were

haunted again and he said, "I had to thank God for not extinguishing Zoe's light."

"I understand." She'd had some choice words for the man upstairs herself, both good and bad.

"And I had to thank Him for giving me yet another chance at life and to say this." Spencer rolled his wheelchair over to the bench where Raina sat. Then he rose up ever so slightly, so he could bend to his knees.

What was he doing? "Spencer, get up. You've just been in car accident. You need to get some rest." Raina rose to help him up, but he gave her a slight push back into her seat.

"Listen up, Raina Martin. I've had about enough of you running away from us. You're going to sit in that seat until I say everything I need to say."

"Which is what?" she asked, smiling, though she suspected she had some idea.

"You sure don't make it easy." He laughed. "But I wouldn't have it any other way." He reached for her hand and brought it to his lips. "I've endured two major car wrecks and if it has taught me anything, it's that life's too short and not to take things for granted."

"I know." Raina tried to interrupt him. "Which is why—"

Spencer placed his index finger to her lips. "I love you, Raina Martin. You've had me enraptured from the moment we met. I know sometimes I've been a caveman around you, but it's because I've known that you're the woman I'm going to marry."

Raina's eyes grew large. Never in a million years had she expected Spencer to mention anything about marriage.

"You're everything I've been looking for, for so long,

but couldn't find. You have beauty, wit, charm, warmth and have sexiness in spades. And I don't want to waste another minute of my life without you. I want you. No, I *need* you in my life. So I humbly ask that you agree to be my wife. Marry me, Raina."

Raina was overcome with emotion. He'd beat her to the punch. She'd wanted to tell him that she loved him and again he'd gone full speed ahead like he always did, but in that moment she didn't care. Tears of joy sprang to her eyes.

"Is something wrong?" Spencer asked.

Raina shook her head, "No, quite the opposite. Because I—I don't think I've ever really told you just how much I need you, too."

"You do?" Spencer asked hopefully.

"I do. You mean the world to me, Spencer. When I thought I'd lost you…" Raina's breath caught in her throat. "I—I thought I'd die. I didn't know how I was going to be able to go on without you."

"You didn't lose me, baby."

"I know, but I almost did. And I can't put this on my parents alone. I put a rift between us because I was afraid of the passion and love you evoked in me. I'd never had it my entire life from my parents, so when you showed it to me, I ran away from the one thing I wanted most, the one thing I'd always yearned for."

"Oh, Raina." Spencer scooted beside her on the bench so he could pull her toward him, but Raina held back.

"Let me say this," she responded, pushing against the hard wall of his chest. "Let me tell you that I love you, Spencer Davis. I love you so much. And I need you in my life, in Zoe's life. And I would be honored to be your wife."

"Raina." Spencer leaned forward and brushed his lips across hers. "My sweet Raina, I adore you."

"And I love you."

Epilogue

"Zoe, be careful," Raina's mother chided Zoe as she playfully rubbed Raina's pregnant belly as she sat on a lounger in her parents' backyard. Raina, Spencer and Zoe had come over for Labor Day barbeque.

"I'm sorry, Mama," Zoe said and quickly rose from the lounger. "I'll be more careful. I don't want to hurt my little brother or sister."

"It's okay, sweetheart," Raina said, but Zoe had already bounded off. She'd been shocked when Zoe had called her the endearment a few months ago. Zoe had long since stopped calling Spencer Spence and had started referring to him as Dad. But Raina had never expected Zoe to call her *mama* and certainly had never asked to be called anything other than auntie. Zoe had said it felt right and had wanted to know if she was okay with it.

Raina was more than okay with it; she was honored. She had some pretty big shoes to fill, but she would do her best by Zoe even though she and Spencer would soon have a little one of their own.

She glanced over at her father and her husband across the lawn. They were by the smoker and barbecue cooking up a variety of ribs, chicken and sausages for the day's events.

After the car accident, she and Spencer hadn't wanted to waste another minute and they'd gotten married on New Year's Eve. They'd wanted to be husband and wife as they brought in the New Year. And they'd brought it in all right because she was already six months pregnant and they hadn't even been married a year yet.

As if he sensed her watching him, Spencer smiled from across the lawn and came striding toward her. "Hey, babe." He bent down to give her a lingering kiss before lifting his head.

"Hey now, that's what got us here," she said, rubbing her belly.

He smiled knowingly. They'd had a lot of fun on their honeymoon and their first few months of wedded bliss. "Can I get you anything? Milk, water or lemonade?"

Raina smiled. "No, all I want is you."

Spencer raised his eyebrow "Oh, yeah?"

"Oh yeah." She gave him a naughty wink. She'd been horny as hell in this second trimester, while her first trimester had brought minor bouts of morning sickness. When she'd thought her lustiness was abnormal, the doctor had informed her it was completely normal so their love life hadn't missed a beat.

"Oh," Spencer said, lying across the lounger next to her. "Then I can't wait to have my way with you later."

"You promise?"

"Do I ever renege on a promise?"

She smiled broadly. "No, you never have."

"And I never will, Mrs. Davis," Spencer said and covered her mouth with his.

* * * * *

A new miniseries featuring fan-favorite authors!

The Hamiltons: Fashioned with Love
Family. Glamour. Passion.

Jacquelin Thomas	Pamela Yaye	Farrah Rochon

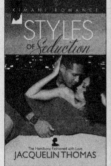

Styles of Seduction	*Designed by Desire*	*Runaway Attraction*
Available September 2013	*Available October 2013*	*Available November 2013*

REQUEST YOUR FREE BOOKS!

2 FREE NOVELS
PLUS 2 FREE GIFTS!

KIMANI™
ROMANCE

Love's ultimate destination!

New holiday tales by
three hot authors…

A Very
Merry
Temptation

Kimberly Kaye Terry
Pamela Yaye
Farrah Rochon

This festive anthology from three fan-favorite authors features new stories about holiday wishes and holiday kisses! Will these couples discover holiday magic that's made to last?

*Available October 2013
wherever books are sold!*

H HARLEQUIN®
TM www.Harlequin.com

KPAVMT1013